Beautiful Enigma

ETHICS OF THE HEART SERIES

SK MASON

ISBN (ebook) 978-0-6452824-0-5
ISBN (paperback) 978-0-6452824-5-0

Cover art by Kate Farlow from Y'all That Graphics
Editing services by Kat Pagan from Pagan Proof Reading
paganproofreading@gmail.com

Mamie, this summer, you and I will be reading again. In my mind, we're in Normandie, sitting on the couch, going through these books and swapping them with each other, ignoring the eye rolls of everyone else. Because we're right. There's nothing better than a happily even after.

Mémé, this might not be as good as 'Angelique, Marquise des Anges', but hopefully we can still take turns at reciting the best lines anyway. I can see us in the dim lights, with Mum and Caroline, crooning over Jeffrey's love gestures.

Blurb

I've found the solution to my problem. He's charismatic, professional, and mine for three days.

I admit I have ... issues... when it comes to intimacy. But at nineteen, I'm ready to cash in my V-card and get the whole charade over with. Between my less-than-stellar childhood and the douchebags who bolt whenever they learn about my lack of experience, the walls around my heart are high. Too high for the silly notion of love.

It's time to take matters into my own hands, or rather, put them in the capable hands of a sexy, high-class escort. It'll be a business transaction. Too bad my heart and body disagree once the Aussie hunk shatters every idea I have about relationships and pleasure.

What happens when two souls who aren't looking for love discover just what a beautiful enigma it can be?

Trigger Warning*: Mentions of child abuse from heroine's past, trauma, and cheating.*

Chapter One

Oblivious to the thousand bodies crawling the Brisbane night club like drunken fire ants, Dylan trails his hand up my skirt, my excitement igniting like wet matches. I moan when his lips engulf mine, just as my best friend Jess does with her beaux of the night.

Fake it until you make it, sister.

Jess's voice grows louder in my head with every new move from my boyfriend. She'd be proud of me. Virgin or not, by the time I learn all the tricks of the trade, Dylan will be none the wiser.

Heavy, warm breaths blow inside my mouth, and I force my eyes shut, wondering how on earth people get turned on by this. It's fucking pathetic. Draining. It's the equivalent of walking on hot cinders.

Making out next to us on the couch, two girls giggle as they fondle each other's boobs, bumping into Dylan's tongue-sucking marathon in the process. As grossed out as I am by the PDA around us, I thank God for the interruption.

"Want a drink?" Dylan asks, his eyes following the trail of hot bodies bopping on the dance floor of The Prohibition.

"Yes, thanks." As soon as he disappears into the crowd, I glance at the time on my phone, and sigh when only a measly hour has gone by since Dylan, Jess, and I stepped into the club. It feels more like a week.

Across from me, Jess waves, then kisses some guy on the cheek before she dashes to my side. The couch creaks as she leans back. "Raven, sweetie, tell me this isn't awesome?" she asks, as her hands pump in the air with every beat screaming in the background.

I roll my eyes and blow a hard breath. "Nope. I'd rather be in bed."

An alcohol-fuelled finger taps me on the nose. "Now, now. Remember," she slurs, "Dylan is not any random guy. He's a local god." She taps my nose with every next word, like she's typing morse code. "Fame, popularity, money."

Qualities which could erase the image of the poor girl, tainted by her family's domestic violence and questionable choices once and for all.

She continues, "He has everything, and you'll want to claim him before any of these bitches try to steal him off you."

I slap her hand down, mouthing 'sorry' to the girls narrowing their eyes at Jess's digit twirling in their faces. "Stop it. You're gonna get yourself in trouble, girlfriend."

"Are you going to consider my vibrator plan A, or are you sticking with your outrageous plan B?"

My head falls on the cushion behind me, shame rolling through my stomach. "Ugh." This isn't a conversation I thought I'd ever need to have. Not that nineteen is old, or that being a virgin at nineteen is a crime, but in this day and age, admitting that I'd never even been kissed until a few months ago generally leads to some really curious looks.

"Fine. I'm guessing the dildo is still a no-go. Why don't you just tell him you're a virgin, then?" Jess asks, her head leaning against my shoulder. "I think you're hot. I'd have you."

Because as hot as he is, he doesn't strike me as the talk-therapy type.

"How much have you had to drink?" I deadpan, while patting the top of her thigh.

"You're not Stella. He wouldn't make fun of you like that."

I squeeze my phone a little tighter, my palm hoping to erase all the screenshots that have leaked through campus in the last couple of weeks between Dylan and his friends.

Laughing. Dissing. Pitying some poor girl who lost her virginity in a lust-induced oblivion. I'm not sure what shocks me the most: the amount of blood staining the sheets, or the fact that for these guys, taking someone's virginity was a chore.

Apparently, experienced women are not only less messy, but they also do all the work.

"I'm not risking it."

She shrugs. "Okay, but pretty sure Casanova expects some ass very soon."

"Don't make it sound so vulgar." I shake my head, cringe-worthy frustration hitting me. "He's hot. He's smart, and he's funny. I could have scored worse."

"He does everything for you." She wraps her arms around me until her voice is but a murmur in my ear. "Except turn you on."

Oh, Jesus.

My best friend might be right, but it isn't on him. Dylan has a hot body, and all in all, he truly is every girl's dream.

It's not his fault.

I've tried to get myself off. In the dark, in the morning, with fingers or with the showerhead. The most I've felt were slight tingles, but never the earth-shattering explosion everyone talks about. And yet, that is an upgrade to what I feel when Dylan kneads my flesh like yesterday's bread.

No. The issue is me. I am frigid. Untouchable. Unlovable.

Like my father yelled at my mother a hundred times: some women are just as cold as ice, and fucking an ice cube is bound to freeze your dick off after a while.

I sigh. "Nothing turns me on. It's not him, so might as well get the V-card out of the way, learn a few tricks, and dazzle him once I've learnt to fake orgasms like a porn star."

Jess rotates towards me, her eyes narrowed like a grandma without glasses. "Are you telling me that you've never had an orgasm? Even by yourself?"

A couple of bodies turn towards us, and I rush a finger to her lips, silencing her. "Shhh, don't advertise my brokenness to the world for Christ's sake."

"Like anyone can hear above the music." Her eyes roll at the obvious.

Based on the vibrations rocking us on the couch, she has a point. I concede and move closer until my mouth touches her cheek. "Never had one. In all honesty, I'm starting to think that the big-O is just a big ol' myth."

Her eyes grow wide, her mouth contorting as she stares at me from head to toe. "A hot babe like you?" She picks up a strand of my hair, the long red lock dancing through her fingers. "With these bright blue jewels we call eyes, no way. You just haven't tamed your sex appeal, sister."

My cheeks burn, and I shake my head. My best friend's clearly buzzed. "Everyone is hot when you're drunk." I chuckle.

"Nuh-uh." She lowers her eyes to my boobs. "Look at the size of these puppies." Her hand palms my tits. "Perfect shape."

A smile curls my lips, my brain giving up on having a grown-up conversation with my friend. I'll have to confirm plan B by myself. How bad of a plan could it be when it came professionally recommended by my therapist, right? "Okay, sweetie. I'm a super-hot catch. Everyone knows that."

Behind me, a familiar voice interrupts our girly heart-to-heart. "You are definitely a hot little number, sweet pea."

I snap myself back and force an awkward smile as Dylan runs his tongue behind my ear.

It's enjoyable. It's enjoyable. It's enjoyable.

"A hot, sweaty bod I can't wait to have naked under me." My boyfriend drops a few shots in front of us and points to the guy Jess was smooching. "Left Romeo by himself?"

My best friend salutes him. "Sure did. I'll get back to him later." She rolls her shoulders slowly until her neck pops under the pressure. "Or his friend. I'm not fussy."

Dylan raises his hand to fist pump her, but she narrows her eyes and shakes her head with a sour look on her face. "Nah, I'll pass. Not too impressed with these screenshots going around town. I'd be a piss-poor feminist if I pretended to approve."

A slight blush creeps up his neck, but he ignores it and instead, completely leans back against his seat, some weird pride taking over the confrontation. "Hey, you got to look at it from our side, sister. If a girl's gonna mess up a dude's bed like that, the least she can do is warn him."

"Warn him?" I ask, my voice a little pitchy.

My boyfriend grabs my hand, then drops his lips to my knuckles. "I get all girls have to go through it, and I'm happy to help the next gal out, but at least let me run a sheet of plastic over my bed and jerk off beforehand so the lack of action doesn't give me blue balls."

My jaw drops, my heart rate spiking in my chest.

Is that what I have to look forward to? Quick deflowering over a builder's sheet as a favour to mankind?

Jess straightens, her sobering pretty instantaneous. "Tell me, stud, have you ever considered, let me think..." She pauses in an exaggerated huff. "...that making love was about... love?"

Dylan tilts his head like she's grown a third eye. "Love?

Come on, Jess." He points towards the back of the club where a bunch of hotties are gathered. "Would you rather fuck some green newbie, who won't know the difference between your clit and your ass, or get fucked good by one of *them*?"

She rolls her eyes, her lips tight. "You're a jerk, you know that?"

He laughs, then launches his mouth in the crook of my neck and drops a bunch of wet pecks. "I'm a jerk who loves real women. The ones I don't have to initiate by having them suck my dick." He downs one of the shots, eyes closed, and adds, "And before you think I'm the only guy who thinks like this, praise the good Lord you ain't virgins anymore, cause I'm just one of many who'd rather spare the carnage."

My throat tightens at the vision in my brain, and I fight really hard to keep the tears at bay. I inhale, counting to five before releasing my breath, a fake smile on my face. By the sound of things, faking will be my middle name for years to come, so I might as well embrace the role.

Dylan hands us a shot each. The blue and yellow colours float in front of me before I scull it as fast as I can. And when he slides a hand between my knees, I smirk and open them up for him a little.

I might be condemned to a life of unsatisfying sex for the rest of my existence, but I sure as hell won't be anyone's pity party as they do me the favour of bleeding me like a butcher's wet dream.

Resigned to save what's left of my dignity, I search for the small business card in my purse like it's a second-chance joker. I don't need to see it to visualise the black and gold cursive letters. I already know what it says, and I relax as my thumb runs over the edges of the small cardboard.

.   .   .

Aussie Paradise - Male escort service.

Your safe, friendly, and respectful neighbourhood hunks.

Plan B it is.

Chapter Two

I stare at the white building in front of me while my palm lingers on the door handle. I flinch when the frosted glass swings open, but armed with my big-girl panties, I plaster a smile on my face and step towards the reception desk.

What kind of escort service has a freaking marble counter?

It's not just the reception desk that throws me off my game. No. It's the twelve-foot ceiling, the soft music playing in the background, and the café, bar, and tub chairs entertaining a bunch of equally gorgeous people.

Staff or clients?

I scan the room, eyes wide, nodding at the security guard who grins my way as he prompts me forward. I smile politely and let my feet glide over the pristine tiles through the massive foyer.

Nothing looks as I'd pictured. Not that I was particularly jumping at the idea of getting my V-card stripped by a middle-aged sugar daddy, but this place is Hollywood worthy. Not quite the 'good enough' service I had in mind.

"Welcome to Aussie Paradise," a woman in her midthirties says. She rearranges a Chanel scarf around her neck before she grabs a clipboard from the desk. "I'm Natalie. You must be Raven."

"That would be me." The attempt at deflecting my nerves must be very underwhelming, based on the pursing of her lips that follows.

"It's lovely to meet you," she says, then twirls an index finger in the air. "Don't be taken aback by all of this. I promise you this is the best place to have a good time."

I fight the blush creeping in, the heat spreading from my neck to my cheeks. By the time Natalie has stepped around the counter and is standing next to me, I'm drowning in my own sweat. "That's, uh, reassuring, I guess."

Oh god, shoot me dead.

Frigid *and* stupid. Jackpot.

The woman grabs me by the elbow until we're both settled in a small room (more of a nook, really) in front of a bunch of catalogues displayed on a glass table. A topless hunk smirks at me from a laminated page, and I force my eyes back on my hostess as she straightens paperwork in front of us.

"Aussie Paradise prides itself on offering a professional service to men and women who want something a little more special than a quick hookup, minus Chlamydia, as part of the package."

She snorts at her own joke, and I sit there, mouth gaped, wondering why the fuck I've never contemplated *that* before now. A part of me considers bolting, but my feet are anchored to the floor, my butt stuck in the tub chair like yesterday's spaghetti Bolognese.

Oblivious, she continues, "Here's how things work. You take your time perusing our Aussie hunks. And when you've picked your *crème de la crème*, you let me know, and I'll set you up for a fifteen-minute complimentary introduction." She taps the catalogue in front of me. "We pride ourselves in matching our customers with the right escorts, and both have to consent to the match before we go any further."

So far so good.

I nod, my shoulders dropping. I wipe my palms on my jeans and relax when my stomach finally settles. *John* stares at me from the first page of the booklet, pearly whites inviting me to read on. This twenty-three-year-old stud is a romantic at heart and would like nothing more than the opportunity to sell me a full-night package to galivant across town before making love to me.

I grimace and move on to the next one. I don't need a romance package, and there'll definitely be no lovemaking. Based on Dylan's gruesome and descriptive tales, I'm guessing it doesn't take that long to deflower a girl. The plan's a quick in and out. Get the job done. No deep dive into my eyes as I die of shame through the ordeal, and definitely no faking about how amazing it felt afterwards. Hell, I don't even plan on giving them my name.

Natalie urges me on, and I turn to the next page, my fingers shaking against the glossy paper. My next option, *Sam,* sends me a smouldering look so deep I wonder how the book hasn't combusted by now. His package includes a breakfast-value meal.

"Sorry, can I ask about these packages? It seems that there're quite a few..." I clear my throat. "...options."

Natalie smiles and places another sheet in front of me. "We cater for all types of encounters." She points to the list as she gives me an overview. "From a single night to a full week."

I'm guessing Aussie Paradise doesn't rent a room by the hour?

As if she read my mind, she adds, "Don't worry about the package options right now. This gets negotiated between you and your match during your intro." She winks. "After all, you might want more after you get a taste."

I struggle to keep it together, my throat tightening. I scan through the next three pages, and dismiss Peter, Paul, and Murray, wondering if this is a fucking joke. I'm expecting someone in a lab coat to take me out back to harvest my organs any minute now. My heart rate skyrockets. My head grows dizzy, and the drumming in my stomach resumes. My fingers dig into the armchair as I rise to my feet and ask, "Could I use your bathroom?" And as soon as she points me in the right direction, I dash.

The water's cold on my face, and I wait—faucet on—by the basin until I feel like a human again. A couple of women storm in. Pink cheeks. High heels. Like they're on actual dates. They flutter in the bathroom like two teenagers.

"God, it's like he gets better and better every week," a blonde wearing a dark cocktail dress croons at her friend.

The brunette by her side brings her laced fingers under her chin and bats her eyes in an exaggerated fashion. "They don't call them hunks for nothing, sister."

Together, they giggle, nodding briefly in my direction as they wash their hands on each side of me. "Hi," the blonde says. "First time?"

That obvious?

I lift my gaze to the mirror, and cringe at the beads of sweat running down my face, my hair stuck in thick chunks to my forehead. "Yep." I fake wash my hands for what seems an eternity while letting my fingers rearrange the red curls into something a little less farm-like.

"The first time is always weird, but once you find your match, you'll never bother with real-life douches." The brunette shakes her head like she's trying to forget the bad ending of a B-movie.

I cough, mustering the question in my mind. "Any recommendations?"

"More of a wishful-thinking type." Her finger gravitates

above my head, until it taps the poster of another candidate on the wall between us.

'For a limited time, get acquainted with Jamie' the sign says, and a guy in his late-twenties smiles at me. Unlike the others so far, his black hair falls in locks over his forehead, and he's wearing an actual shirt that moulds the body of an athlete.

"He's the one everyone wants to sample, but the man is *sooo* picky." The blonde pouts. "His stats say less than five percent of intros move forward."

This time, I take a good look at Jamie, curiosity pushing me past the bundle of nerves threatening to have me bent over the porcelain bowl. There's something about him that doesn't scream *meat market.* He's attractive, but wrapped in a down-to-earth blanket that oozes a cocktail of safety and confidence. All he's missing is the cherry on top.

That cherry of mine, she wouldn't mind him doing the honours.

My body's still shaking, but since there's an important job at hand, I'm voting it gets done by the big blue eyes staring at me. With a renewed conviction, I make my way to Natalie, my stride a little more assertive.

"I think I'd like to meet Jamie." I close the catalogue left open in front of me and push it towards her.

"Jamie?" she asks, her perfect smile faltering. "He's certainly a brilliant choice, but..." She centres the hunk bible between us again. "...on extreme demand."

I only need ten minutes, lady.

"I don't expect to need much time, and I'd appreciate it if you could just set up an introduction?" The puppy eyes must have worked, because within a minute she's got Jamie on the phone. And apparently, I can have an interview—I mean an introduction in the next thirty.

Natalie leaves me in the café, my tummy doing summer-saults as I wait for the guy to show up. In front of me, the condensation drips from my glass, and I run a finger over imaginary lines, my brain screaming a thousand contradictions.

Pack your shit and leave. Relax and enjoy the ride. Plan B was really fucking stupid.

Parched, I close my eyes and suck on the straw. Sprite cools my insides, until I hear it—the chair opposite me scraping across the floor. My eyes open slowly, and there he is. My Aussie hunk, in a black suit, like he's just escaped from an important business meeting. Perfect teeth grin back. Deep blue eyes, sparkling as they scan me briefly. And lips, plump lips that glisten as he leans over the table and hovers above me. Without breaking eye contact, Jamie gently pulls the straw out of my mouth and slides it straight into his.

He takes a long sip, before pushing my soda between us again, then says, "Hello, beautiful lady. Care to share your name?"

Chapter Three

"Veronica." I stumble over the name, trying hard not to visualise my year-six teacher as I introduce myself (or not myself) to the guy sitting in front of me.

He winks. "Is that what we're going with?" He slides a form between us, his smile reaching his deep-blue eyes. "That's cool. I love role plays."

Glancing towards the piece of paper, I cringe at my info clearly spelt out, embarrassment locking me into my seat. How hard can it be to hire a gigolo for an hour these days? This place is so proper. Everything is above board. At this rate, they'll have my tax file number and charge me full taxes.

I sigh, skipping the justification that I'm brain-dead, shame-fogged, and have no idea what I'm doing. To his credit, he drops the topic before leaning back, one arm wrapped around the top of his chair as he waits for me to recover.

He's hot. I can see why he's in demand.

Our friend Jamie is incredibly buff. Athletic. Strong. As if the blue eyes contrasting with jet-black hair weren't panty-melting enough, he sports something of a charismatic confidence that lights up his face every time he opens his mouth.

"Thanks for meeting me." I take a sip of my drink, my throat loosened enough that I can start forming coherent words again. "You come highly recommended."

He tilts an imaginary hat off his head and bows, a silver chain around his neck undulating as he leans in towards me. "We try our best to please."

My jaw drops, the reality of where I am smacking me in the face. *Oh my god.* My heart rate triples its speed, and I force a deep breath into my lungs—Jess's plan A suddenly doesn't sound so crazy. Though, a vibrator won't teach me the tricks I need to master to keep Dylan happy and oblivious to my lack of sexual desire.

"That's... good."

Jamie squares his shoulders and with a smile, he asks, "Tell me about yourself, *Veronica*?"

I tilt my head, my face etched with confusion. "About me?"

"Yes, sweetheart. Look around you." He gestures to the immaculate building and matching professional atmosphere. "We're in the business of making people feel good, in and out. And to do that, I like to understand what it is women need from me."

I nod and wait, like a schoolgirl listening to her hot teacher's instructions.

"Sex is lots of things, and it's different for everyone. What is it for you?"

Heat radiates from my face, and I fight with all my strength not to bury my head in my hands. These women weren't kidding when they called it an interview.

I waver between faking a blissful libido and telling Jamie the truth. In the end, I surrender to the obvious. He'll have to know at some point anyway. It might as well be now, while I'm still wearing clothes and staring at the emergency exit sign a couple of metres behind us.

I straighten in my seat, wiping my sweaty palms on my thighs, and brace for my confession to get to a new level. "Sex is nothing to me. Can't say that I've ever got off before."

My glass slides across the table until it's in front of him and he's sucking on the straw again.

I continue, hiding my slight irritation at him for finishing my Sprite. "I have this amazing boyfriend—Dylan." I grab a sugar packet from a bowl in front of me and let my fingers roll the contents from one end to the next. "But he's very experienced, and he'd prefer an experienced woman."

He chokes on the drink, eyes wide. "Are you telling me your boyfriend sent you here so you could get better in bed?"

The sugar powder rolls faster in my fingers until the paper is thinner than a baby's hair. "Not quite."

He cocks an eyebrow and motions for me to keep going.

"I'm not exactly orgasm friendly."

"What the hell does that mean?" he asks, curiosity turning his eyes into deep-blue sapphires.

Jesus. Will he just spare me?

I puff, hot air deflating my lungs, and blurt out, "I can't climax."

He shakes his head. "Don't tell me he's one of those guys who takes that personally?" When I remain silent, he chuckles. "Worse, huh? One of those guys who can't work out how to pleasure a woman?"

I hide my face in my palms, and every atom in my body fires at my predicament. If I admit to him that I'm the defective one, I could lose my plan B. If I don't, I'm only going to delay the inevitable and have to relive this awkward exchange, but the second time, it will be in my underwear.

"Dylan and I..."

I flinch when the overworked packet rips open and the white powder flies over the whole table. But when I rush to sweep the contents towards the centre of the glass top, panic threatening to spill, Jamie grabs my hand, forcing me to meet his eyes.

They're kind. Warm. Patient.

"Raven," he murmurs. "You're safe here. You're in control. Relax."

A weird sense of comfort takes over, and I don't recognise it. Nor do I recognise the butterflies stirring in my belly. But it's enough for my brain to prep the words, and they launch from my mouth like bullets. "I'm a virgin. I've never had sex, never had an orgasm, and I want to get it over with."

Jamie's healthy glow takes on a slight pale tinge. "Hang on a minute. You're telling me that instead of preparing to have sex with the guy you love, you'd rather give some random that privilege?" He shakes his head like he's just been slapped. Or like I've said something really stupid.

"Not every guy thinks it's a privilege," I snap.

"And those guys are fuckwits, if you ask me." His bicep twitches as he assembles little piles of sugar in the middle of the table. When the poorly timed dispersal has been contained, he lifts his gaze and our eyes meet before he smiles, like he's dropped his professional curtain again. "What I mean is: sex is special. Whether it's purely for pleasure, as a sign of love or liberation, I'd hate for you to wish you'd saved that moment for someone who cares about you."

Small shards of ice penetrate my blood vessels, and I tighten the cardigan around my body.

Jamie's right. I know what Dylan and I have isn't love, but it's not to say it won't be down the track.

"It's complicated. I know my request is odd, to say the least."

Jamie wrinkles his nose. "Yeah, I must admit… it's not one of my routine requests."

"I'm sure it will take you less than five minutes to get the job done, Jamie. I'm not asking you to save me or to change my life." I clear my throat, my eyes avoiding his. "Just to help me fix this virginity problem and send me on my way."

Jamie nods, a sudden emptiness in his gaze. "So, let me get this straight. You're asking me to fuck you quickly?"

"Yep."

"I don't have to make you come?"

"You couldn't even if you tried."

He rolls his eyes, then adds, "And basically treat this like a clinical exchange with zero work on my part, and no pleasure from yours?"

Finally, it looks like my hunk got the memo. *Simple as pie.* "Yes! That's exactly right. Nothing more. Nothing less."

His eyes glow with some unspoken emotion. And then, like a child who's had enough of a game, he crosses his arms and says, "No fucking way, but thank you for meeting with me."

Did my plan B just bail?

Shocked, I struggle to clear my head, and grab his wrist as he stands up to leave. "Please, if it's about the packages, I'll pay whatever."

"Raven, baby, you're missing the whole point of this." With his free hand, he drags his chair over and sits back down, shifting closer until his face is right next to mine. "This is about pleasure."

A thousand pins and needles crawl up my skin when his lips connect with the crook of my neck.

"It's about consent. The exchanging of ourselves…" He brings his mouth above my ear and murmurs, "Safety."

Like a slow fire that comes out of nowhere, something stirs in my lower belly, and I sink deeper in my chair, the foreign sensation clouding what's left of my frontal lobe.

He glides his hand over my thigh as he leans in, and then I feel it. The connection. The buzzing. Some weird excitement.

I feel it through the beating in my chest, the drumming in my ears, the prickling of my insides.

His lips are on mine within a second, and like a hatchling's instinct to follow the moon, I close my eyes and welcome him. His kiss is slow. Unhurried. Like he's serving some deity, and that goddess is none other than me. A tiny moan comes out of my throat, and I grip his shirt, frozen when I don't recognise my own voice.

What in the holy hell is happening?

He moves back until our eyes fuse with each other. His, glistening like he's as affected as I am.

"I don't fuck women. I share moments with them. Respectful, consensual." He tucks a lock of hair behind my ear and adds, "Pleasurable. Anything less than that, I'm not your guy."

Eyes shut, fist clenched around the base of his shirt, I swallow hard, deep emotions threatening to bubble to the surface. "I'm new at this. You won't get any pleasure, and I don't know how much mess I'll make."

A hand covers mine, the pad of his thumb stroking my flesh slowly. "You don't worry about any of that stuff. I'm a pro. I've got you."

I chuckle, my mind still reeling. "I can see why they call this place Aussie Paradise."

"The one and only."

A voice sounds from behind us, and before I have time to get my bearings, Natalie is sitting at our table, a clipboard nestled in her arms. "I'm afraid we've run out of time for today's introduction." With a smile, she slides her board and matching pen in front of me. "All I need from you is a decision on a package option."

I lift my eyes towards Jamie and wait for him to speak. My hands are shaking; my stomach is flipping backwards. And in all honesty, after this weird moment, I'm starting to think maybe my name is indeed Veronica.

"Please?" I whisper.

He turns his head towards Natalie, and they exchange a glance, like they've done this a thousand times. All business, and as if I'm no longer sitting in the room with them. "She'll take a three-day package. And don't bother with those shitty breakfast vouchers from last time. I expect something a bit better."

Her grin cracks into laughter, but she agrees. Then she turns towards me, sliding a brochure forward, where she's scribbled a bunch of options. But all that stands out is the price underlined in bright pink. "Welcome to Aussie Paradise," she says.

I gasp, my breathing hitched.

It looks like I've just spent $2499 on a three-day weekend, in order to finally become a woman.

Chapter Four

My stomach in knots, travel bag in tow, I step inside the Aussie Paradise building for the second time this week, and check in for the next three days, as per the very thorough instructions Natalie emailed me yesterday.

Check in. Like I'm going on a beach holiday.

The whole thing feels surreal, and there's a part of me that questions whether my organs *are* truly safe. From the agency's 'suggested' bring-along items, to the very strict 'no electronics' policy, my fingers are still trembling after I've signed on the dotted line and retrieved my credit card from the lady at the front.

Room 2A.

The magnetic latch unlocks, and I step inside a modern, self-contained apartment. A large mirror welcomes me, followed by a series of black and white wall lights, abstract paintings hung between them. In front of me, there's an open kitchen. A giant fruit basket awaits in the middle of the counter, not far from a large screen mounted on to the wall, just the right distance from a corner lounge that looks like it was delivered this morning.

My eyes trail the warm sunrays invading the living area, and I freeze at the incredible view out the life-size windows spanning the entire wall.

Almighty God.

Shoes off, my feet sink into the soft carpet, and I cross the couple of metres separating me from the Brisbane River. I brace myself on the black windowsill, feeling insignificant against the life buzzing in the city below.

"It's beautiful, isn't it?"

I pivot towards the voice, and Jamie's standing there next to me, one elbow against the frame. In a crisp white shirt. His hair gelled back. His eyes are filled with wonder as he stares at the view like he's seeing it for the first time.

I nod, speechless. This place is truly something. We stand there for a minute and then, like an excited child on Christmas morning, he grabs my hand and pulls me towards another room. "Let me show you around. You'll love the bedroom."

I giggle as he drops himself on the bed, his body bouncing off the soft mattress. He settles against the headboard, feet crossed, and pats the empty spot to his right. "Don't worry, Raven. I won't touch you. We still have a contract to get through before I'm all yours."

My heart skips a beat. I'd almost forgotten why we were here.

"OMG, check this out." I dash into the open bathroom, and a huge corner spa sits at the back of the enclosed space. A shower, double basins, and a toilet with privacy screens finish off the en suite attached to the love bird's nest. "Imagine taking a bath in there," I hum, eyes closed, visions of the peace I'd snatch in an effort to escape the rest of my pathetic life dancing in my head.

Heaven.

"Why couldn't you?" His voice resonates low in my ear, and warm fingers trail my bare shoulders.

Startled, I meet his eyes in the mirror, my reflection frozen as his body's moving dangerously close to mine. My throat seizes up, my back tenses, and I smile some clunky take-a-step-back grimace that doesn't seem to deter him. "Because you're here?"

He kisses the top of my collarbone. "That's sort of the idea."

My muscles ache from the tension concreting my limbs into place. At this rate, turning into salt would be an upgrade to how I'm feeling right now.

Where the fuck is the rule book?

He places two strong hands on my shoulders. "Raven, tell me, what are you feeling right now?"

Don't you dare tell him the truth.

I swallow hard, words stumbling out my throat like I've been gagged for a week. "Feeling great. Thanks for asking."

"Yeah?" He lowers his head until his mouth touches the sensitive space behind my ear. "Why don't you tell me how you really feel?"

Panic builds inside me. First, it's slow, and for a second, I almost convince myself that he won't see through my lies. But then, my vision blurs and all I see in that goddamn mirror is my colour draining with every stroke of his finger. "Nothing. I feel nothing."

Tears well up in my eyes, and I shift on my feet, mentally counting how many steps there are between me and the door.

His thumb taps the artery pulsing at the base of my neck. "No, Raven. What you feel right now is fear." He gently forces my chin up and guides me closer to the mirror. He towers behind me, and envelops me with his arms. "And I want you to know: you have nothing to fear with me. Not naked. Not with your clothes on. Not ever."

A tear falls on my cheek, and I gasp at the emotions filling me. Anxiety. Shame. Confusion. All of it put together as one.

Overwhelmed, I don't know what's happening to me, and in that moment, all I want to do is run.

"Feeling nothing is what happens when you try to hide what's really going on."

I shake my head at his comment, the depth not quite what I expect from an escort, and march into the room where I settle on an ottoman at the foot of the bed. Jamie follows my trail. He mirrors me, elbows on his knees, and together we wait there, silent, as I'm processing the storm in my mind.

I'm not afraid. Why would I be? It's not like anyone forced me here.

My eyes roll with enough sass that I'm able to regain some semblance of control. Back straight, I deadpan, "I must have missed Natalie's gun to my head, Dr Phil, 'cause from where I'm standing, I'm paying a lot of money for this booty call."

A smirk lifts his lips into crescents, and he leans into his seat, the seriousness on his face vanishing. "All right, Ms Roberts." He winks at the *Pretty Woman* reference, and adds, "When you're ready to talk about it, we can."

I give him an even bigger eye roll and chuckle, my conscious mind busy repacking the vision of my father, watching porn on his phone in the middle of the loungeroom, in the box labelled: sex is fucked.

Sorry, Jamie. You ain't fixing that shit.

Jamie clears his throat and leaps to his feet, before pointing towards the door. "I'll tell you what, why don't we make ourselves comfortable in the living room, and get over the bureaucratic aspect of this *getaway* before all the fun begins?"

I narrow my eyes, confusion dancing in my head. "Okay?"

"The contract." He laughs. "Boundaries, expectations, safe word. That type of stuff."

I tap my forehead with my palm, fighting the chortle brewing in my belly. "Do I have to call you *sir*?"

Tiny dimples form as he leads me out of the room, but he

doesn't confirm nor deny whether I should expect the red room of pain next on the list.

Fifty Shades of Aussie Paradise rules, it is.

The couch sinks with our weight, and as soon as Jamie bounces back, he pours us a couple of pink fizzy drinks.

I twirl the purple stirrer in the glass before bringing my lips to the exotic liquid. "Mmm. It's nice. What is it?"

"Non-alcoholic French Grenadine." He opens a small folder on the coffee table. A couple of forms get shuffled between us, before he adds, winking, "Getting the guests drunk without consent is one of the many things Aussie Paradise frowns upon."

I clap my hands and bring the neatly typed document to eye level. "That should be fun." I cross my legs and lean back against the lounge.

Jamie mimics my posture and switches on some ambiance lighting. Then he clears his throat, sporting his best serious-teacher frown as he starts reading, and I chuckle at his impression.

"Rule one: For the next three days, no phones or computers." He narrows his eyes at me in an exaggerated fashion. "It's to save you the temptation of reselling my nudes online."

A swarm of bees begins to buzz in my stomach at the imagery. My shoulders drop, feet crossed on the coffee table, as I wait for the next rule. Jamie's eyes light up when he sees me relaxing against the couch, and I blush when he catches me staring.

God, he's good at this. If he's as good in bed as he is person-able, I think I might even be able to get through this without horse tranquilizers.

He continues, "Rule two: We are expected to debrief every day on your experience, so that the service can be tweaked to your needs before the end of your stay." His lips wobble like he's fighting a grin. "A one-star review would damage my self-esteem beyond repair."

My cheeks hurt from smiling. For a minute, I wonder how anyone can be both charismatic and funny at the same time. Clearly, that's why he costs more than my monthly wage.

"Do I get a refund if you're not worth the five stars?" I tease and take a sip of my mocktail, excitement building for the next dot point on his list.

"Baby, I'm worth so much more than that." His glass meets mine and he lets them clink together. "Okay. Rule three: All contact is consensual and will require guest approval at every level of intimacy."

I tilt my head, a lopsided grin on my face. "As in, you'll ask me if I agree to any touching before you do it?"

He shrugs. "Yeah, we canned the body cameras last month. Apparently, it got too formal."

I explode in amusement. "Verbal consent it is, then."

"That's it for the fun rules." He shuffles on the couch until his thigh brushes me. "Now the serious part, Raven."

Just like that, the Jamie I met at the café is back, depth lacing his pupils. My heart rate speeds up, and I can't tell whether it's due to the proximity, or the topic at hand. I take a deep breath and relax when my lungs obey my instructions.

Jamie rubs his thumb over the pulsing in my vein. "Good girl," he murmurs. He waits, smiling until it's almost back to normal. Then, he continues, "I know you think you have one goal. But I'd like to explore a few more."

"I gathered that," I say, my tone shaking. I know where this is going... Losing my virginity is why I'm here. Learning a few tricks, definitely a good outcome. But the idea that I could experience pleasure, *that* concept is completely foreign to me.

And a waste of time.

He exhales and drifts towards me until I can feel his body temperature against my chest. "I can make you feel things you've never felt, Raven. If you just let me." He tucks my hair away from my collarbone, his mouth now lingering on the flesh.

Panic sets in, and my muscles tense along with the dread that fills my belly. *Frigid girls don't feel things like that.*

"Will you let me show you?"

I swallow thickly, my body unsure. A part of me considers letting him try, but the other part scoffs at the inevitable ending that's sure to rear its ugly head.

Been there. Done that.

He leans in until I can hear his breath right above my ear. "All you have to do is say yes."

The word comes out before I've even processed it. Like a subconscious wish. "Okay," I whisper.

"Thank you." His tone is soft, like my own security blanket. "Just follow the sound of my voice."

I'm about ten seconds from hitting my imaginary 'fuck off' button when Jamie's forehead leans against mine, and he says, "Stay with me, Raven." Slow pecks trail my shoulder. "Focus on your senses now. I want you to tell me what you can hear."

My brain filters through my mental fog, and I make myself focus on his voice. "Traffic," I whisper. "The air con."

Strong arms lift me, then I'm propped against the couch in the perfect angle. I shimmy up until Jamie's chest cradles my face.

"Now, touch around you. What can you feel?"

The internal battle continues, two forces arguing against each other. But as I feel Jamie's forearms twitching around mine, something shifts. My mind zones in on the present. The way he feels, the way he smells, and the way his voice sounds so close to my ears.

My body quits the fight, and like a rubber band that breaks after years of tension, I fall against him, some weird warmth comforting me. The fear is gone. The apprehension is dead. All that is left is what's happening in this exact moment. "I feel you. Your arms. The tickling of your hair against my face."

He presses his lips behind my ear, letting his tongue caress my skin.

"Your tongue is wet," I say, shock in my voice as I feel no disgust. "But it's warm at the same time."

"Stay right there, baby. You're doing great." His hand travels to my hair before agile fingers work their way through my locks.

I gasp, my body going limp against the cushion. And I smile, my eyes closing as Jamie rubs my lips with the pad of his other thumb.

His breath gets warmer as his face touches mine. And like some weird involuntary reaction, my hands grip onto his biceps as he whispers in my ear.

"Raven, do you consent to me kissing you?"

Chapter Five

Heat pools in my lower belly as I process Jamie's question.

Do I want to be kissed by him?

Based on how fast my blood is pumping, there's no denying that a pretty vocal part of me wants him to. "Yes," I say, though I don't recognise the sound that comes out of my throat. My voice is laced with shock, surprise, and *anticipation*.

"Good." His tone vibrates against my skin. "Because I want to."

He wants to?

A thousand thoughts run through my head like a crew of Skylines on a busy highway. I must have heard wrong. Why would he want to? It's not like I'm good at this.

The chattering in my brain dies down as I focus on my senses, just as he asked—and oh my god, does he smell incredible. It's warm and spicy. Intoxicating. I sigh, and let my fingers grip him tighter as he lowers his face.

All resistance futile, I let him in.

His lips are warm against mine. Light. Like butterflies on a spring day. First, he nibbles at the flesh, until his tongue enters my mouth slightly. And then he waits, as if he's coding my body to brace for more. My lips open. My tongue meets his, and before I know it, I have my palm at the back of his neck urging him on.

What in God's name is happening?

Sweetness invades my mouth. Damp, but dry at the same time. Nothing like Dylan's soggy smooching that dumps truckloads of saliva down my throat.

No. Jamie is gentle. Yet, there's a confidence about his kiss that has me melting against him. I want more of whatever the hell he's doing to me. My jaw relaxes. I push my tongue a little deeper, and when I do, Jamie's touch intensifies. First in the kiss. Then in the way he grabs me. And finally, in how he trails the outside of my thigh with his hand. A tiny moan escapes my throat. A fucking *moan*. I'm confused. My body alternates between burning with every stroke, and freezing with every move. It's intense. Frightening. Unbearable.

And I love it. And hate it. And I hate that I love it.

Time speeds up. The world around me spins faster until I have my calf locked around the back of Jamie's knee. And like a demon possesses me, I bite his bottom lip right before it clicks that I'm wet. Drenched. Underneath my Aussie hunk.

Fuck.

I'm engulfed in a cyclone of strange feelings that have me out of control, but when a burning pinch has my clit screaming for some weird need, I cave to the *eject* button in my head.

My palms are anchored on Jamie's pecs. "Wait," I say, breathless. "I need a minute."

Jamie nods, a genuine smile lighting his being, but he doesn't move. "How do you feel?"

I inhale as deeply as I can, this weird throbbing having yet to subside. "Confused."

He chuckles and lowers his gaze. "I can tell."

My eyes trail his, and my jaw drops. *You've got to be kidding me?* I have Jamie locked—no, pinned between my legs. One calf has his knee hugging mine, while the other has his pelvis secured against me. *Against mine.* Like I'm some horny teenager in a dry-humping spell.

I flinch back, my legs dropping, while all the heat in my body gravitates to my cheeks. "Oh, Lord."

Jamie halts my hand from covering my face. "Raven, stop. Stay in the moment. Send your BS shame and whatever other negative emotions on their way, and tell me what you physically feel right now."

I swallow hard. If I knew how to do that, I would have done it a long time ago. But the fire in me still burns, and it's almost painful. So, if he can make sense of it, I'll take the stud's wisdom. "I feel a mix of pain, and…"

"Pleasure," he mouths, before shifting his pelvis just above mine.

I bite my lip to stop sounds from coming out of my mouth.

"This mix of pleasure and pain." He waits for me to close my eyes and relax before he adds a little more pressure against me. "It's good."

"Oh god, I can't deal with this," I whimper against his forehead. "Is this supposed to feel like this?"

"Yep. When it's done right."

"Shit. I don't even know how to answer this." My hand squeezes the top of his shoulder, and I let my head fall back on the cushion holding us.

His smile matches mine, and we catch our breaths for a second. But then, his pupils darken even more, and he says, "I can make the burning stop. Will you let me show you?"

My heartbeat travels to my throat, and I stiffen, *the unknown* crippling me again. "I don't know what to do."

"You don't have *to do* anything. Just close your eyes and focus on the sensations. Stay in the moment. That's it."

I swallow hard, unsure of what he plans to do. But I nod, the curiosity wanting to kill the pussy cat. Or in this case, I guess it's my literal pussy—*in the hands of an organ-harvesting god*. But, since my brain won't turn back on, I grip him as I stand on the edge of some moral cliff.

He kisses me again, his mouth travelling to the base of my neck, and he adds, "I need your consent, Raven. You have to say it."

"Show me."

Green light in tow, Jamie lowers his hand to my waist. And in a move that could be compared to nothing short of magic, he has my jeans unzipped. His fingers are over my panties within a second.

I flinch, my hand tightening around his wrist.

No one has ever touched me there before.

My breathing quickens. A mix of fear... and undeniable desperation. I'm torn between wanting the slow burn to ease, and being scared shitless of what it is I'm feeling.

"The second you want me to stop, you let me know."

His fingers push my underwear to the side, and I gasp when I feel his skin on mine. Panic fills me. When my eyes shoot open, he's smiling, his hand fixed in place, like he's waiting for me to catch up.

"Relax. I've got you. We're just experimenting. Discovering how good it can be." His voice is soothing. Safe.

My legs fall to the side as his thumb finds my clit and circles it. At first, slowly. Then a little faster. Pressure mounts. I whimper against his ear, my fingers digging into his forearms. My body tenses, some electrical current sparking my vagina in all the right places. "It's so intense."

"Yes, it is." He adds a little pressure until he has me

moaning out loud. "It's okay to experience pleasure, Raven. Tell me what it feels like."

My throat thickens, new emotions building. I focus on the man next to me. His solid frame. His confident stance. His enticing smell. The whole damn package. "It feels good. I feel like I'm going to explode." I almost cry the words, and like Jamie's pushed me into another gear, I grind back and forth against his hand.

"Good girl. You're hot. You know that?"

Jamie's dick hardens against my thigh as the rubbing continues.

"Oh god." My thighs quiver and open wider for him.

"I'm going to put my finger in you now. Okay?" He's kissing my throat, his tongue teasing the special spot behind my ear as he warns me.

"Please," I whimper, before I feel his thick finger stretching me. Bit by bit. Until he's thrusting in and out, soothing every nerve dancing in my vagina. "Jesus Fucking Christ. Don't stop."

I can see what everyone is carrying on about.

The intensity climbs until my heart is pumping through my chest like a jackhammer. My whole body is drenched with sweat, and my mind's as clouded as a drunken sailor post-hangover.

Jamie has his thumb worshipping my clit while his middle finger, buried in my depths, makes me squirm. The pleasure is unbelievable. It's beyond my control now, and I force my eyes shut as my body is on the verge of falling.

Fuck it. If pleasure is bad, then I'm bad. Because this is something else.

"Let go, Raven."

"Jamie!" I cry his name as pins and needles spread through my core.

Maybe I'm not frigid anymore.

Frigid. Like your mother.

By the time I've recognised his pathetic voice, the mental cold shower has shattered my buzzing, and it now feels like someone's stitching my cervix with a ten-gauge needle. My father's cackle fills my ears. And I harden, the reminder that women are either sluts or useless in bed screaming in my head. And he's right. He's right about women. And he's right about men having needs: the need to fuck, or the need to get paid to fuck.

Like a sex worker doing his job.

My eyes open, tears welling along my lashes. And I clench my teeth, praying to God that the escort who's finger-fucking me for a paycheck won't notice.

"I think I'd like to stop now."

As soon as I say the words, Jamie's off me, his blue eyes questioning. "What happened, Rav?"

I leap to my feet. Confusion, anger, and shame lace what's left of my dignity. How stupid was this whole plan anyway?

"Nicknames? I must have missed that in the rule book," I snarl. I swallow my tears, my throat throbbing, and I march towards the bathroom. In the end, Dylan, Jamie, or Dad. They're all the same. Men don't care about women's pleasure. It's either their entitlement or their job. "I'm going to take a shower."

I ignore the glum tinge on Jamie's face as he nods politely while he tidies up the couch. And as fast as my feet will take me, I insulate myself in the darkness of the bathroom. The door closes behind me, and I'm alone with my dread.

If the price of experiencing pleasure is the humiliation that follows, then I don't want it. Instead, I'll scrub Jamie off until all I feel is nothing again.

Chapter Six

The water's as hot as I can bear it, the steam drowning my lungs as I steady myself against the shower tiles. I scour my arms and legs, red trails marking my skin with every swipe.

You're so pathetic.

A soft knock startles me on the other side of the privacy screen, and I ignore it. Instead, I scrub harder, facing the stream head-on until the water in my ears almost drowns out Jamie's voice.

"Raven?" His tone is deeper, hesitation marring his regular self-assurance. He waits a minute, and when I don't respond, his steps get louder until his voice literally vibrates through the plastic between us. "I need you to tell me that you're fine."

The bathroom lights come to life, and my eyes narrow until they've adjusted. "I'm fine. Happy? Could you turn the lights off on your way out?"

"Of course. I'll give you some time." The lights dim. "Let's chat when you're out."

I don't need to fucking talk about it, mate. Move on, already.

I smack the tap, cold air blowing on my skin as soon as the

stream dies, and I stomp out of the cubicle. The hotel towel is around me for no more than thirty seconds before my legs slide into thick leggings and a matching hoodie.

It's not like I'm going for sexy right now.

I toss my hair in a messy bun and climb on top of the king-size bed. Legs crossed, my back settled against the headboard, I finally let out the breath I've been holding. I exhale, my shoulders dropping. But it's short-lived, because within a minute, the bed sinks under Jamie's weight.

He swipes a hand over his face, then matches my posture until we're both resting against the bedhead, staring in front of us, legs straighter than a couple of toothpicks.

"I guess now's as good a time as any to debrief." He sighs. There's hesitation in his eyes as he taps both thighs with his palms, like he's searching for a new rhythm. "Is that okay?"

I clench my jaw and smile. A smile as fake as Jess's lips. "And what if I don't consent to that?"

A despondent chuckle bounces from his diaphragm, and I pinch myself before I start feeling sorry for him.

He exhales and pivots until he's facing me. "Daily debrief. Sorry."

Mouth tight, I roll my eyes. "Of course. It's in the contract."

"Raven, even if it weren't in the fucking contract, I'd want to know what happened."

He shifts, his body completely opposite mine now, and there's an urgency to his tone that I don't recognise. As far as I can remember, it's not like anyone has ever asked before. Or cared. Though it's not his fault, the change in gear leaves me lost. My throat stings, and I ignore the nails digging into my palms, my mind chanting to focus on the present.

What? We're following this therapeutic advice now?

"I'd like to understand what happened so I can make sure

it doesn't happen again." A line deepens his forehead. "If I've done anything to hurt you, or even upset you, I'm sorry."

"Don't worry about it." I wish I could talk about this abundance of crap. But in all honesty, if I started, this three-day getaway would turn into a lame midday show, sponsored by a truckload of complimentary Kleenex. Not quite what Aussie Paradise is aiming for.

Jamie lowers his voice and says, "You were with me, and then you weren't."

Inside my body, a storm brews. It starts from my toes and travels to the tips of my fingers until all my limbs feel numb, and I have no choice but to answer, or leave. Because as it stands, it's like he's in my head. All he's missing is the popcorn before he sits down to watch the film of my shitty life.

Who is this guy?

The taste of metal fills my mouth, the inside of my cheek paying the price for Jamie's laser-focused questioning.

He waits for me to answer, and when silence fills the air, he asks, "Who were you with?"

My chest heaves, my nails clawing deeper into my hands, and I fight the adrenaline shaking my body. The room temperature feels like it's dropped, and I struggle to adjust to the psychosomatic shivering. I wrap myself in a tight hug, hoping that maybe a confession is all I need to purge the bastard out of my head *for good*.

In one swift move, Jamie's pulled the spare blanket folded by our feet and wrapped it around my shoulders. His hands grip onto the fabric as he tucks me inside the material, like a newborn swaddled tight. It's a welcoming warmth that soothes me, even just for a minute. And it's enough to give me the strength to exorcise the elephant in the room.

"My father," I blurt.

Jamie opens his mouth to speak but doesn't. Instead, he

tightens the blanket around me and leans back against the bed. "I'm sorry."

"It's not like he touched me or anything," I explain. Though, according to my therapist, his outbursts and inappropriate choices of words and entertainment around me weren't much better.

"There're no levels of hurt, Raven. It's not a competition." He places a hand on my back. "All pain matters. You matter."

My head tilts and I'm speechless. How does someone respond to *that*?

Small fissures crack my resolve and my inner cold-hearted bitch melts, while Jamie sits here in complete silence as I expunge the million thoughts running through my head.

It's not my fault my father discussed my mother's bad lay at the dinner table. Not my fault he'd insist that his porn mags remain in the bathroom at all times, and definitely not my fault he professed that we needed to either learn to cook or suck a dick properly—if we wanted any hope in hell of keeping a guy.

Tears well up in my eyes. "Sorry." I shuffle until my legs are crossed under me and my arms are nestled inside the blanket, like a childhood ritual against the monster under the bed.

I don't even know why I'm considering telling this complete stranger things I haven't even told my counsellor. Maybe it's the way he waits for me to be ready. As though he knows I need to let it out. That somehow, I'm done with being afraid. Done with expecting the worst, and done with running from hope. Or maybe he senses... that for some reason, I just want to.

Jamie's eyes study me. They watch the way my hands pull the blanket tighter, the way my lips wobble as I decide how much I'll say, and the way my chest heaves up and down as I take deep soothing breaths.

What I don't know is why.

Why does he care?

"I'm not used to..." I wave a finger in the air. "...this."

He smiles at my awkward chuckle, but it doesn't quite reach his eyes. "Have you heard of cuddle therapy?"

My neck twists at a perfect ninety-degree angle, the move worthy of a scene out of The Conjuring. "Hmm. Can't say that I have."

He leans back against the headboard, ankles crossed, and lifts his arm into an open embrace. My eyes grow wider, and I stare at the empty spot against his chest. Without blinking. My heart drums into my ears, so loudly that I can barely hear the next words that come out of his mouth.

"Raven, do you consent to me giving you a hug?"

Against all common sense, I nod, and he pulls me against him, laughing. "Come here, then."

A fresh minty scent takes over my senses and I inhale as deeply as I can, my brain going on overdrive. He smells like walking through a rainforest on a spring day. I close my eyes and let my face rest on his chest, as I visualise imaginary sunrays kissing the surface of my skin.

"Is this okay?" I whisper.

He cradles me into a tight hug. "It's more than okay."

My palm crawls up until it's resting against his stomach. A soft heartbeat pulses through his shirt, and it vibrates until it settles beside my cheek. It's warm. Welcoming. Safe.

Foreign.

"Do you do cuddle therapy with all of your clients?" I murmur, my soul still surfing in the quiet part of my mind.

His hand rubs me back and forth. "No."

"Why me, then?"

He sighs. "I have no idea. But it feels good, right?"

"Yep." My thumb trails the ridges of his abs, each groove a new discovery. His stomach is tight, his temperature warm, and there's something soothing about touching him while knowing he expects nothing more. "Thank you."

He plants a kiss on my forehead and leaves his hand on my back, his heartbeat slower than before.

When I open my eyes next, the room is dark, and Jamie is spooning me under the thick doona. I stiffen, then relax when I realize we're both still wearing our clothes. His breathing quickens as I stir, and he shifts to his back, his arms stretching above my head.

"Can't believe we fell asleep." He yawns.

I turn towards the clock on the bedside table, the time lighting the screen. "It's almost two AM. It's been hours!"

He turns to his side, his eyes heavy with sleep. "We're on holiday. Just relax." He pulls me back against him until I'm cradled in his arms. "Please tell me you like sleeping in, right?"

I chuckle. "Who doesn't?"

"My year-ten girlfriend," he mumbles. "She thought six in the morning was it." He stretches deeper this time, as he cocks an eyebrow. "And why are we still talking?"

"Because I'm awake and I need to pee." I laugh and dash to the bathroom.

When I come back, Jamie's eyes are alert, and there's pink lemonade waiting for me. Next to the glass, he's propped a couple of chocolate biscuits.

"I guess we're definitely awake now." He chuckles as he straightens. "I have an idea," he says. "Since we're up already, wanna play a game?"

Chapter Seven

A *game?*
Jamie's playfulness is contagious. Or maybe it's the grin. Either way, I've agreed before I've even checked that it's not strip poker.

"As long as I win, I'm good."

He laughs at my comment, grabs a pillow, and shoves it behind his back, propping himself up.

"Hey, I'm the guest. That should be my pillow." I grab the corner of the cushion and wrestle him for it.

The stunned glaze in his eyes tells me he didn't expect my playful assault, and the object of my pursuit is in my hot little hands before he has the reflexes to stop me.

"You wish," he yells.

Within a second, I'm flat on my back, and he's hovering over me, the pillow long tossed across the room. Our eyes meet, and his grin morphs into something else. His arms box me in, his face right above mine. His lips twitch as he scans the way I bite my bottom lip.

"What's the game?" I rasp, my throat drying.

"Truth or dare," he murmurs back, but neither of us move.

"Truth."

He smirks, holding my stare, and rolls to his side so he's braced on his elbow. "What do you do in life?"

Hope to break the cycle.

"Digital marketing student. Second year."

"Nice. Enjoying it?"

I nod. "Yeah. It's the way of the future," I sing-song while motioning for his turn.

"Truth. I'll play it safe for now." He waits for me to ask my question.

I narrow my eyes. "How old are you?"

"Twenty-seven," he says without missing a beat. "An old man, compared to you."

I explode in laughter and run my hand through his jet-black locks. "Yep, the grey hairs don't help your cause."

He closes his eyes, a small smile on his face, and I let my fingers travel through his mane as he leans against my palm.

"Why are you doing this?" I whisper, my mind wandering through the *Alice in Wonderland* rabbit hole of what it would be like to have a Jamie by my side. Maybe he's different. Maybe he's right. Maybe there are some good men out there, and I've just been lumped with a shitload of A-holes who don't deserve to represent their whole gender.

"Because it feels good," he purrs, his lips stretched to his ears.

I shake my head. "No, silly. Why the escort job?"

"Ah. The one-million-dollar question." He waggles his eyebrows. "I take on assignments for one month a year."

"What?" I gasp, louder than I meant to. "What do you do the other eleven months?"

"I probably shouldn't tell you," he teases. "Groupie and

all." He laughs when I smack his forearm, and then he continues, "I'm a business consultant."

I straighten, legs crossed, my mouth opening wide. "What do you mean a business consultant?"

Jamie stretches his hands behind his head as he laughs again. "You didn't see that one coming, did you?"

My jaw's on the floor, waiting for a Tonka truck to pick it up. Heat warms my cheeks. "No. Sorry."

"Why does it seem so impossible?"

Jamie gives me a small smile as I pick at imaginary lint on the pillowcase between my legs.

"I assumed this type of work was about the money."

And it's not like I wouldn't get that part.

He shakes his head, no signs of tension in his body. "Nope."

A chuckle tickles me as I picture Jamie booking his fuckathon once a year like most people plan snow trips. "So, why?"

"Dare," he says, avoiding my question. Instead, he tucks a strand of hair behind my ear, and winks. "Come on. Make it spicy."

My palm slaps my forehead, the provocative invitation not exactly subtle, and I narrow my eyes at the Aussie hunk.

Dude, being a virgin doesn't make me a prude.

"Take your shirt off," I instruct him.

He pauses, like I've surprised him, and a twinkle in his eye glows as he gets on his feet and slowly unbuttons his shirt. He's in front of me, back straight, eyes checking to see if I'll bail.

The cotton slides to his shoulders, and he lets the shirt sit there, front open to perfectly crafted abs. Small black hairs line his stomach and disappear under the belt of his pants, and I fight my eyes from travelling below, wondering if the rest of him is as gifted.

The bed creaks as I kneel on the mattress and face him. Jamie waits, smiling, then pulls me closer to him as he guides my palms against his collarbones. He's warm. Hard. Like he's made of concrete that's soft on the inside.

A feeling of safety buds from the pit of my stomach. It's small, but it's there. Like a dim light in the middle of the night. Jamie oozes respect. In his eyes. In his tone. In the way he takes his time. And experienced or not, and as strange as it may sound, it's as though it's okay to be me.

Below my fingertips, his heartbeat pulses faster. My hands crawl over his chest like I'm crafting my first clay. I take my time, feeling the strength of his shoulders as his shirt falls below his forearms, then I uncover the thickness of his pecs, his abs, and his waist hiding underneath the white material.

A deep breath fills my lungs as we exchange a glance. He lifts his hand, and his thumb traces the pulsing in my neck. I gasp as his fingers linger there.

"Your turn," he says, without breaking eye contact.

Don't be a coward.

"Dare," I murmur.

"Good girl," he whispers in my ear, his breath forming a trail of goosebumps against my skin. "Take yours off."

I hold his stare and smirk, as I pull the hoodie over my head. Within a second, I'm standing in front of him in a cotton bra. "I'm not scared of a little competition."

His lips lift into crescents. "I'm glad." He runs his fingers over my bare shoulders until we have both of our hands on each other. "Remember: the second you want to stop playing, we do, Raven. Okay?"

Warm tingles run through my body, and tiny zaps of electrical current hold me hostage against quitting now. My hands run over his chest with a little more direction, like they're trying to memorise its shape. The shape of my own borrowed Adonis.

"Kiss me," he says without moving an inch.

He waits for me to decide, and as if we're suspended in time, neither of us speak. Instead, I drift closer to him, our chests touching, and inhale the scent of pheromones until I'm drunk on the guy. I close my eyes as my senses awaken to him. His smell. His skin. His touch.

With every stroke of his fingers on my arms, a crescendo builds. And I give in. The way he licks his lips as he stares at me, the slow running of his hand on my stomach, and how much I want his mouth on mine all have the neurons in my brain firing at rapid speed.

Butterflies flutter in my lower belly, and I recognise the stirring forming again. My heart skips a beat, and I hesitate. His eyes locked on mine, Jamie freezes, his body moving back a fraction. And he squeezes my hand, his fingers laced with mine.

"Focus on what you feel," he murmurs. "Only that." His thumb strokes the top of my hand.

Something in me shifts, and when my father's voice pipes up, I hurl it to the pits of hell, my fucked-up emotions halted, and make sure they're locked deep in the do-not-dare-disturb corner of my consciousness. As if the shackles of my mind have snapped, I'm hungry. Like I've been starved for the last two decades, and the man in front of me is who I want right now.

I launch myself forward, and he welcomes me against him. Our mouths connect, and as though driven by instinct, our tongues dance in sync. For a second, I lose track of time. The world spins, leaving Jamie and me in our dimension, kissing, nibbling at each other's lips until the warmth that has engulfed me burns in all the right places.

"Touch me again," I tell him.

"Is that really what you want?" His voice is deep as he lowers me to the bed.

I pull him closer to me. "Please."

His hands stroke my stomach gently, his fingers warm against my skin. He's cautious. As if I'm worth a thousand diamonds. Precious. Like I matter to him.

I stare into the blue of his eyes. They stare back at me, a shade darker.

Maybe he's like this with all of his clients, and turning himself on is one of the many perks of the job. The thought crosses my mind, but I push it away because the truth is: right now, I don't fucking care.

"Raven, do you consent?"

"Take my clothes off." I grab his face and kiss him until he has no doubts that this is what I want. *Need*. "Show me more."

He pauses, a deep breath filling his lungs. "Fuck," he groans, his eyes trailing my body. In one swift move, my pants sit in a pile at the bottom of the bed, and I'm lying in nothing but a bra and knickers under Jamie's watchful eye. "You're beautiful," he says, a finger running over my breast.

My nipples harden at his touch, and I inhale, bracing for the foreign sensation. "God." I chuckle. "How do people handle these feelings?"

He hovers over me, a grin on his face, and settles between my legs. "Baby, it's going to feel even better when you're ready. Right now, you know the drill."

I know. Focus on the present.

My fingers rake his hair, and he grunts when I pull it. The sounds coming from him do something to my ovaries, and another gear shifts when he sees it on my face. With his foot, he pulls my ankles apart and my knees lift until they're hugging his thighs. His mouth trails my neck, leaving warm kisses from the back of my ear to the top of my breasts. I'm on fire. My hands fist the sheet, my calf hooking him closer to me, and I squirm, pressure building inside my core.

His hand dives into my bra until he's freed the flesh from its prison. Then, one by one, he cups my breasts, like he's appraising something valuable. And he hums, as he alternates between licking my hard pebbles, and flicking them with the tip of his fingers. I feel it in my chest, between my legs, and most shocking of all, in my mind.

The freedom. The confidence. The safety.

The sensations build, and I don't know how long I can handle this sweet agony. I unbuckle his belt, and Jamie shuffles out of his clothes until he's wearing nothing but boxers. His hand runs up and down the length of my thigh. Slowly. Like a well thought out torture plan.

When his fingers reach the lace of my underwear, I jolt, a thousand megawatts begging for relief. "Please," I moan, "I can't hack any more of this."

He kisses me on the mouth while he slides my underwear off. "Stay with me."

I'm not going anywhere, champ.

His finger glides over my folds, up and down, first on the outside, and then teasing my slit until I'm writhing underneath his hand.

"You're so wet," he groans into my ear, as he keeps his finger teasing me. "So. Fucking. Wet."

I swallow hard, turned the hell on by his tone. It's husky. Assured. *Needy.* Almost as much as I am. "I want it inside me, Jamie."

He closes his eyes, his bottom lip between his teeth, and takes a deep breath as he pushes his middle finger further.

Oh god.

Pleasure builds with every one of his thrusts, my legs spreading wide, and I quiver when he starts palming my clit. His body tenses as I moan against his chest, and he pushes his finger in and out, faster and faster, until I have both hands gripping onto him.

"Jamie," I whimper, growing afraid of the intensity building around me.

"Let go, beautiful. I'm right here with you."

His voice is clear. Assertive. Guiding me towards a new level of amazing.

His mouth lowers to my breast, and he takes in the whole nipple. He sucks on the bud, licking it, and when his teeth scrape at the skin, my legs stiffen, my body convulsing in a thousand beats around his fingers.

"Oh god." I pant in the crook of his neck as shivers take over me, and I'm flying through the most intense experience of my life. It's an explosion of the body and mind. It drains me of everything. My limbs grow limp, free of any thoughts that go beyond how fucking incredible this feels. "Don't let me go."

Some weird emotional buzz grabs me, and I grip onto him, seeking his warmth and reassurance, vulnerability whipping me hard.

What the hell is going on?

His body hugs mine as he lets his hand rock my wetness until the throbbing quietens down; then he kisses my forehead as he tightens his hold on me. "Not going anywhere, baby."

Chapter Eight

J amie hugs me tight as I'm overcome by shivers and inexplicable feelings. "What's happening to me?" I chuckle as I curl into his chest. I'm hot. I'm cold. I'm overcome by a mix of ecstasy and shame all in one, and the cocktail is flirting with my sanity.

Strong palms rub my arms, as Jamie hums next to my ear. "You're okay. Stay with me. It's just a little sub-drop."

I lift my chin. "Sub-*what*?"

How much training does one need to have sex around here?

"It's your body's way of coping with the intensity." A grin fills his face. "What comes up must come down." He sways us on the bed, and whistles. "And holy fuck did you go up."

I sink deeper into him, his heat hiding the blush creeping up my face. His heart beats fast. It throbs almost as forcefully as mine. "Never heard of it." Not that sex is my favourite topic of conversation, but I would have thought someone would have mentioned it. Like Jess, or the hundreds of articles on preparing for the deed I've read in the last week.

It seems like nothing could have prepared me for the experience with Jamie though. I expected a quick lay. Not hours of cuddle therapy as he gets into my head, tearing down one barrier at a time.

Don't get attached. It's only a job to him.

He swipes my forehead and hooks my hair back. "It's a BDSM term we use across the board." He taps my nose with his index finger. "And it makes you even more beautiful."

"Completely exposed, you mean." I exhale deeply, my breath finally catching up to the rollercoaster. I ease back against his shoulder. "God, I'm so relaxed now. Like my body's just finished a marathon."

He laughs. "Just like it's supposed to be."

"Is that what sex feels like?"

"No. That's what intimacy feels like, when two people experience safety and respect. Sex is sex. I can put my dick into anyone, but without the connection, they all end up the same. No damn point to that."

"Is that what it's like when you're working?"

He shifts until his back is propped against the head of the bed and he's looking into my eyes. "No fucking way. I won't take on an assignment unless I connect with the girl. And I won't have sex with her until there's mutual respect."

He's sooo picky...

Bathroom blondie's comment makes perfect sense now, and I grin at the memory. "Yeah, so I've been told. Why did you pick me?"

He shakes his head. "I don't know. I wasn't going to. You're way too..."

"Inexperienced," I utter the single word that seems to haunt me. It makes sense. If Dylan didn't want the chore, neither would a guy like Jamie.

"Precious," he finishes, a darkness lacing his features. "I feel unworthy of having this place in your life."

My fingers link with his. "You're not. I want someone like

you to be my first. I've already felt more with you than I have in my whole life."

He kisses the top of my hand. "Are you scared?"

"A bit. I don't know what to expect."

A caring smile enlivens him. "I won't hurt you. I won't do anything until you're ready for me."

"Will it feel like before?"

He purses his lips. "Probably not the first time. But after that, I'll make sure it does."

God, this man is hot.

His words are laced with promises that do something to my insides. I don't know if I'm still wet from before, or whether it's happening again, but the thought of Jamie fucking me isn't *the worst* thing I could think of.

"Good. Because I'm ready for more."

His eyes grow wide and his lips curl as he processes my comment. "Fuck me dead, woman. This isn't how it's supposed to be."

"How is it *supposed to be*?" I purr in his ear as I slither next to him and straddle his waist.

His hands run over my ass, and he caresses the flesh as he positions me right above his crotch. He closes his eyes, appreciation marking his features, and says, "I'm not supposed to be feeling like a horny teenager."

I chuckle and lower myself until my tits are in front of his face. "It's okay with me if you enjoy it too."

I grab the back of his head and bring it forward until my nipple's locked between his teeth. I arch my spine, a moan building already as my pelvis rocks against him. I dig my fingers into his biceps, a switch in the dynamic flicking. Tension builds in the air, and each part of him grows harder than a Besser block. He grunts every time I move, while his manhood stiffens until his boxers are nothing but a thin veil between us. I grind against him, my wetness seeping through the material.

"Fuck." His abs twitch, and his legs straighten under me. "I want you bad, Raven."

Our lips meet, our tongues rekindling, as our heartbeats thump through the new wave of energy coursing in the room.

I whisper in his ear, "I want you too—*right now*."

He pauses, his breathing erratic. "Are you sure?"

I nod, and within a second, Jamie's hovering above me. There's a flicker in his gaze, a flush to his cheeks, and the hard-on he's sporting leaves nothing to the imagination. He glides a hand between my legs and hums. Eyes closed in appreciation, when it slides in and out, my wetness drenching his fingers. "You're so ready," he murmurs, then kisses me with a new intensity, like something in him snapped and he can't hold it anymore.

I nod, a mix of excitement and apprehension buzzing through my body.

I'm ready.

I've never felt so beautiful, so confident. So *womanly*. I want this like I never thought I would. *Or could*. As if he senses it, Jamie takes control, his body charging mine like a hundred magnets. A foil packet appears on the bed, and he shuffles with it until he's prepped on his elbows above me.

"Give me your hand," he rasps.

My breath hitches when I feel his firm cock beneath my fingers. It's hard. Warm. Hungry for me.

"This is what you're doing to me, Raven." He pins my hands above my head, our fingers intertwined, and adds, "I'll be as gentle as I can. I'll stop anytime you tell me to."

"I trust you," I whisper against his mouth, and swallow hard as Jamie lines himself near my entrance.

Arms shaking and jaw clenched, he hovers over me as if he's trying to slow it down. His eyes are glazed. High. Ready to pop. And finally, with a deep breath, he asks, "Raven, do you consent to me making love to you?"

Making love to me?

"Yes," I whisper, and brace myself for him.

He shifts back and forth in small motions until my body gets tighter, and my virginity's the only thing stopping him. I'm so wet. He spreads my moisture in and out of me with his fingers while flicking my clit in circles till I'm climbing again.

"Trust me. Stay with me, okay?"

"I'm ready," I say between kisses. *As ready as I'll ever be.*

He pushes through, and I wince, the sharp pinch resonating in my pelvis. My breathing grows erratic as my heart skyrockets. "Ah." My body tenses, and I panic, my legs straightening beneath him.

Jamie stops moving. Our eyes meet. He lets go of my hand to run his fingers through my hair. "Hey, beautiful."

My brain buzzes, the comfort in his gaze soothing me as I try to comprehend how a complete stranger has the power to make me feel so appreciated.

I'm safe.

"Hey." My throat is tight.

"The hard bit's over, baby. I'm inside you. Relax for me, and I promise it will feel better now."

I bring my hands to his chest and close my eyes as my body accepts him. Jamie's big. He fills me perfectly, but the sensation is strange. My mind loosens its bridles and the rest of me follows. The tension lessens in my limbs.

"Good girl," he grunts as he eases into me slowly and swings back and forth until it doesn't feel so tight anymore.

I exhale, the burning dissipating. Instead, there's a warmth that spreads every time Jamie thrusts gently between my legs.

When his dick goes in and out effortlessly, he takes a deep breath, the lines on his forehead smoothing. "You feel so good. You're perfect."

A hand behind his neck, I rub the muscle as he shifts in and out. "Don't stop." I wrap my legs around his waist and dig my heels into his ass to pull him closer.

He dives deeper, his breathing growing faster, and locks his eyes with mine. "I won't last if you keep doing this," he pants, his heart rate pulsing through his rib cage. I can feel it against my chest, and a coy sense of pride overwhelms me.

I'm doing this to him. Me.

As the stinging dulls, it's replaced by a stillness, an emotional gratification that empowers me. Gives me full control. I close my eyes, my body taking all he has to give. *Willingly.* And I pull him in closer, my pelvis meeting his halfway with every thrust. "Come for me, Jamie," I order him.

His head snaps up, his eyes widen. "Shit." He clenches his jaw, his body growing taut as he takes heavy breaths and shifts to faster strokes. They're sharp, focused, and they have him groaning until he's convulsing inside me.

"Good boy." My hand strokes his bare back.

His movements decrease, but he doesn't stop. When the tension leaves him, he finds my eyes, lines melting from his face. "I don't even know how to respond to this."

I did this. Shove your frigidity up your ass, Dad.

My fingers continue to stroke his shoulders. "That was hot."

Sweat drips over his pores, his breathing uneven. He falls to my side but doesn't let me go. Instead, he hugs me tight. "Thank you."

Chapter Nine

Did my escort just thank me for having sex with him? Brain-fogged, I stare at him, wondering what I'm supposed to say. Is there an escort etiquette I've missed?

I nuzzle against him, tossing the rule book out my mental window. We lie still, legs intertwined until I register the wetness lingering between us.

God, no.

I flinch, Dylan's warning resurrecting between my ears.

The least a girl can do is clean her mess.

I stiffen in Jamie's arms, humiliation filling me, and wonder how the hell I salvage my dignity from this predicament. My breathing quickens, and I'm frozen in place, visions of *Friday the 13th* rolling in the mental theatre of my mind.

Strong arms pull me closer. "Raven?"

"Yes," I say, eyes closed, fists clenched.

"Get out of your head."

"I can't." Tears well in my eyes, and I fight the voice crack as I continue, "I'm scared to look."

Jamie tosses the tied condom in the waste basket by his side and leans over me. "Look at what, babe?"

"The blood." My voice is as thin as a board. Surely when he sees the carnage, he'll have me billed for a bond clean.

He pecks my lips. "Would you like me to look for us, then?"

I nod, exhaling a deep breath.

Jamie glances down, and the sheets shuffle under his hand. When he lies next to me again, there's no signs of anger. Not in his eyes, not in his smile, and not in the way his body curls by my side. "Would it be unprofessional if I said that all of this turned me on?"

This guy is definitely one of a kind.

I narrow my eyes. "Focus, lover boy. Some of us are freaking out here."

He laughs. "God, I think you need to get a refund from whomever taught you sex-ed." He winks at me as he rubs the top of my hip. "There's a little blood on the inside of your thighs, and no more than a couple of fifty cent coins on the sheets. That's it."

"Sorry." I grimace.

"Sorry? For what? The hot as hell experience?" He leans closer until his mouth reaches my ear. "I'm so fucking turned on by the sinful, animalistic fact that I did this to you. But if you ever tell Natalie, I'll fuck you senseless until you die of orgasmic explosion."

The tension in my belly settles, my lips stretching across my face. "Can you even die like that?"

He laughs. "Don't know. But I'd like to try."

"I'm guessing this isn't the typical professional lay?"

He shakes his head. "Fuck no." A line draws across his forehead, some weird, confused gaze lacing his features. He shakes it off before he leaps out of the bed. "Stay here. I'll be right back."

His voice resonates through the apartment as he mumbles into the intercom. Then, without a word, he's shuffling something in the bathroom, the water pipes rustling in the dark.

I wish I didn't have to go back to real life.

I push the thought out of my head, and chuckle when Jamie storms back in the room, bare-assed, and scoops me into his arms. I rest my head against his shoulder. "Where are you taking me?"

He kicks the bathroom privacy screen with his foot, and we step into a Bali-worthy, day-spa view.

"It might sting a little." Jamie lowers me into a bubble bath, the warm water hugging me in all the right places. There're scented candles spread throughout the room and fresh juice sitting on the ledge of the tub. He presses a button and bubbles come to life behind my back.

"Oh my god," I croon. "Where have you been all my life?"

He splashes warm water over my breasts. "It's nice, isn't it?"

"Hmmm." Silence fills the air, but for the sound of the water splattering between us. "Come in with me." I skim the surface with my palm, and shuffle forward so he has room to fit.

The soapy liquid sloshes over the edge as he squeezes his six-foot frame behind me. "Shit." He laughs. "I'll order house-keeping for tomorrow. We have plans anyway."

"We do?" God Almighty, this weekend is worth every penny.

"Yep. Go hard or go home, right?"

His fingers trace the bubbles on my forearms, and a slight pang hits my chest as I count down the hours until it's time to *go home.* Not that my life isn't great. But for a second, this almost felt real. Like Jamie and I are a couple, and I'm genuinely loved.

"Do you have any more..." I clear my throat. "...clients after this weekend?"

The visions of him treating every other girl this way puts a damper on my mood, but I force a smile as he sinks us lower into the water.

"I'm sure Natalie will try to pimp me out." He chuckles awkwardly. "What about you? Where are you off to from here?"

Meeting Dylan and his deadbeat crew for an afterparty, where I'll try to implement some of my new teachings.

"Meeting my boyfriend on the Gold Coast. By train, since I left my car back home." I shake my head. "Sounded like a good idea at the time. Now, it's fucking idiotic."

Laughter fills the room. On the opposite end of the tub, Jamie's feet tickle mine, until he asks with a serious undertone running through his voice, "Why would a girl like you stick around a guy like him?"

Because that's as good as it gets?

I puff, jumbled thoughts swirling in my gut. "He's not a bad guy." I take a deep breath and push the mixed emotions back to where they came from.

He kisses my shoulder. "When you get out there, don't give yourself to someone who doesn't deserve it."

A stray tear falls on my cheek, and I thank the gods for the fact he can't see my face—*and* for the doorbell that jolts us both.

"Time for the best part," he yells, before he gently moves me forward and gets out of the tub. Once dried, he hands me a clean towel and says, "You have two minutes to get your pretty little ass out and meet me on the couch." A quick peck on the lips, and he dashes out of the room.

This is too good to be true. Don't let this be the anticlimactic moment where my kidneys get harvested.

I'm dressed in a flash, and the second I step outside the bedroom, my nostrils wake me. Hunting for the smell of heaven, I trail Jamie on the couch, a massive pizza box on the coffee table in front of him. He pats the seat to his left, and I spring by his side as he opens the box. The smell is pure ecstasy. The warm aroma of blended herbs and tomato sauce takes over until I'm ready to chomp on the cardboard.

"Oh my god. It smells amazing."

Jamie hands me a huge slice, the soft cheesy dough flopping in my hand.

"Gina's pizzas are out of this world. Try this."

He guides the slice to my lips, and mouth wide, I let my tongue dance around the explosive flavours.

"Hmmmm." I chew slowly, the juices melting on my taste buds. Sinking deeper into the couch, I fold my legs until I'm sitting on my calves as I suck on my fingers, making sure that every bit of it lands in my stomach.

"This, baby…" He points to the pizza box and soda bottles next to it. "…is the epitome of good sex."

I chuckle. "Compliments of my Aussie hunk."

"You bet. Anything else, you tell them to get lost."

"Orgasm, bath, then pizza." I wink at him. "Got it."

He shrugs. "In no particular order." A smirk crosses his face. "I'm not opposed to trying to make you come a second time after pizza."

"Ha." As much as I can't wait to experience another lot of fireworks, the thought of doing it again tonight has invisible heat burning my poor lady parts.

He pecks me, and points at the freezer with the glass of lemonade before he hands it to me. "Tomorrow you won't feel sore at all. But, in the meantime, I have an icepack ready for my new friend if you need it."

My jaw drops. "You're telling me that you got me an icepack?"

He smiles. "Right next to the tubs of Ben & Jerry's."

OMG. My heart swells with how thoughtful he is. It's like being drowned by Care Bears I never knew existed.

Next to me, Jamie takes a massive bite of his slice. He rips the dough with his teeth and has finished two more before I've even consumed my first one. A drop of tomato sauce glistens on the side of his mouth, my eye catching the shiny trickle.

He's beautiful. Inside and out.

My fingers lift and close the distance to his face. Slowly, my thumb swipes the corner of his mouth, and our eyes lock. His hand grabs my wrist and keeps it there, his chest rising, and he sighs. "What are you doing, Raven?"

I cross the space between us and bring my lips to his. "Getting out of my head."

He nods, small lines crinkling the sides of his eyes. "You're an enigma, Raven." Then, he tosses his pizza on the plate and launches at me, his kiss laced with passion. "A beautiful enigma."

Chapter Ten

The aircon hums in the background of Jamie's Audi, radio hits playing softly through the console. The guy has taste. Leather seats, dual air, sunroof, and in addition to all the top-notch accessories, the black sedan's roomy. I have my legs fully stretched in front of me, my elbow cradling my head against the tinted window.

"Okay, next guess. You lose this one, and you're unredeemable." Jamie's fingers brace his temple in a shooting gesture.

I bring my hands to my mouth, pressure mounting as he's counting down from thirty.

You're getting your ass kicked.

"How am I supposed to know? I probably wasn't even born." When there's no sign of sympathy on his face, I change my tactic. "Give me a clue, lover boy."

He throws me a quick glance, the corners of his mouth lifting before he trains his eyes back on the road.

There's a youthful demeanour to him. Maybe it's the black tee that moulds his abs, instead of the usual suit. Or maybe it's the aviators that hide the depth of his stare. Either way, there's another layer of hotness behind him, and I'd be lying if I said it didn't worsen my brain fog when it came to Jamie's pop quiz trivia.

"Last one. It's in a movie." He clicks his fingers to get my attention. "And you were definitely born."

"You wouldn't know. You're way older than me," I tease, and smack the top of his thigh. Before I have time to pull my hand back, it's pinned under his, and he laces his fingers with mine.

"Focus, child. That's all you're getting from me."

The song resonates in the car again. I scramble, trying to put the lyrics in every context under the sun. And right when he's about to reach the end of his countdown, I laugh and cover his mouth. "Stop, stop. I've almost got it."

"As much as you had the other ten?" He kisses the inside of my hand before he gently places it back on his thigh.

"Okay. Fine. Tell me," I cave.

He's much better at trivia than I am. The man's not all body, clearly. His brain's just as enticing. As soon as he knows he's won, the corners of his eyes crinkle and his mouth lifts. There's a glimmer of excitement in his voice as he baritones "Kiss from a Rose" for me.

My eyes follow the shadow of the ocean as we drive through the New South Wales border. "Where are you taking me?" Kilometres of deep sea chase us as we climb quiet roads, leading to even more incredible views.

"It's a surprise."

I narrow my eyes. "We already had an amazing brunch. You're telling me there's more? All part of the Aussie Paradise package?"

He shakes his head. "Nope. It's part of the Jamie Kendrick package."

My neck twists faster than a lightning bolt until I'm completely facing him. "Did you just tell me your full name?"

He laughs. "I guess I did."

"Wow, I feel special."

He smiles at me, a twinkle glistening in his eyes. "You should."

Is this what intimacy feels like?

Something fizzes in my stomach as Jamie's words sink in. My teeth nibble at my bottom lip, and I fight my brain from reading too much into it.

Making people feel good is his job. Stop with the gooey eyes.

"How do you know so much about songs?"

He taps the steering wheel with his index fingers rhythmically. "Will you judge me if I said it was one hundred percent drunken SingStar?"

It's hard not to laugh at the visuals, and based on the grin on his face, he knows that.

"The only bad part was my cousin Emma insisting on picking the most depressing songs by the end of the night. We'd lose the will to live, after listening to her interpretation of the freaking Titanic theme song ten times in a row." He fakes a shudder. "That girl should have been banned from drinking."

Picturing him with a bunch of cousins is hilarious. "Ha. All right. Play your worst song. I'm sure I can win at *that* game."

He grins. "You're on. If you get three out of three, I'll rescind your worst-trivia-player-ever title."

Game on.

When the first song plays, I roll my eyes at him. "Really? Is that all you've got?" The guy has no idea how skilled I am at recognizing depressing ballads. After two decades, it's on my CV in capital letters.

I relax against my seat, my grin growing by the second. He's got no hope in hell.

He cocks an eyebrow. "I'll believe it when I hear it. What is it, Miss Musically Crippled?"

"*Say Something*, Christina Aguilera." That's an easy win. I close my eyes and listen to the lyrics, her sadness poking at my chest, before I dismiss that lame attempt. "All right. Next?"

"Fine. Let me find a harder one." He fiddles with the console until the next tune plays.

Goosebumps lift the hair on my arms as "Don't Speak" filters through the speakers. Of course, I know it. I let the lyrics fill my head, remembering all the times I'd wished people'd stop talking around me, and keep their bullshit reasons to themselves every time they hurt me. My mood dips a little, but I paste a smile on my face as I give him my answer. "No Doubt."

He slaps the steering wheel. "Damn."

"Last chance," I tell him as a little part of me curses the stupid idea. I can't say that I'm feeling super uplifted in this moment, but I push the emotions away, and wait for him to select his new title.

He tugs his bottom lip between his teeth, and puffs as he presses play on the screen between us. "No way you're getting three out of three. Give it your best shot."

The melodic ballad chimes in the car, the piano keys hitting hidden spots in my heart. It's like I wrote it, and my smile is a little forced as I look at Jamie. What I really want to say is that one day, I won't need to be afraid because of *anyone*. But instead, I just give him a straight answer. "*Because of You*, by Kelly Clarkson."

His head jerks towards me, a competitive grin swallowing him. "No way. How does this happen! I was winning."

His laughter is sweet, and I love that he has no idea of the turmoil I've self-inflicted, so when he challenges me to a last game, I don't bail. Though, I probably should.

"All right. Final round. You pick your worst, the most depressing song you've ever heard, and if I don't know the words to it when you play it, I'll crown you the winner for the day. Only today though," he teases.

I hum, digging into my musical memory. Truth be told, there's one song, but I'm a little afraid of hearing it right now. "One. But it *is* depressing."

"Let's give it a go. What's it called?"

"My Immortal."

He purses his lips. "Shit. I don't think I know it. Or maybe I do, but I'd have to hear it. Don't give up on me yet."

He presses the voice control in the car software, and once he's asked the android auto to search for it, the song begins to play.

And instantly, I know this was a mistake. The song always triggered me, but after the last fifteen minutes of bleak foreplay, I'm climaxing through my PTSD before the first bar of the melody.

My soul recognises the rhythm before my brain has time to register the lyrics. My heart skips a beat. It might have been a long time ago, but when the first words of the song swirl in the space of the car, I remember it all.

The shame. The pain. The hopelessness.

With Jamie here, his warmth is cracking at my walls, and I'm afraid. I'm afraid to live the rest of my life the way I've lived the last nineteen years.

A sharp pain slices through my insides, and I know instantly that my ghosts are as alive as ever.

Who the hell were you kidding anyway? Things like this don't go away.

Goosebumps lift my skin, my throat tightening until I feel like I'm suffocating, and I gasp for air, a soft cry shaking me. I bring a knuckle to my mouth and bite into the flesh as I've done a hundred times before. Except this time, I'm not hiding underneath the staircase, praying to God my father doesn't find me. Instead, I'm in an escort's car, and it's Jamie who's staring at me as I unravel the darkness my mind's packed and repacked a thousand fucking times before.

It's that damn song.

"Just ignore me," I tell him. "Body memory. I've got a few choice memories with that song I'd forgotten about." I attempt a lame chuckle that falls flat when Jamie pales and pulls the car over.

In one second, he's on the passenger side, the door wide open, and he's lifted me into his arms. He cradles me on top of his bonnet, and pivots until we're staring at the Kingscliff view. He presses his lips to my forehead, his skin clammy, and whispers in my ear, "I'm right here." Another kiss lands on me. "I don't care what's happened, and if anyone hurts you again, it's me they'll deal with."

Sobs shake my body as my fingers claw into him, gripping onto his shirt until his voice is all I hear, like a small light in the darkness. I close my eyes and focus on the way his arms shield me, the way his voice soothes the slashes carved deep into my soul, and the way he hears me even when the words don't exist between us. Jamie's a stranger to me, and yet, he makes me feel things that I've never felt before.

He rubs my back slowly, his face hidden in the crook of my neck. "You're being reborn, Raven. Let him go. Let them all go."

Blue waves hit the thousand-year-old rocks in full force until they crash against it, disappearing like they never were. In the distance, a pod of whales follows each other in complete silence, oblivious to the beauty around them. Warmth spreads as sunrays kiss my skin, and I inhale, the sea-salt air cleansing my wounds as I cradle in the embrace of this beautiful stranger. Above us, the wind rustles through trees, like a quiet lullaby.

"I'm sorry," I whisper.

Jamie wipes my cheek with his thumb, then he gently lifts

my chin until our eyes meet. "Don't ever apologise for letting yourself be vulnerable around people who care."

He cares.

I straighten in his arms, and he loosens his grip. Then my feet touch the ground, and we're standing against the hood of his car. "Sub-drop, right?"

A tender smile flickers on his face. "Something like that."

"It's beautiful," I murmur as I glance at the view in front of us.

He nods and snakes his arms around my waist. "I grew up around here. As kids, we'd come here after school and dive from over there." He points to rocks a few metres below us.

When my breathing settles, he pulls my hand towards the beach as he clicks the remote of his car. The sedan bleeps behind us, and within a minute, my feet sink into warm sand and we're strolling on the dunes. A couple of dogs chase each other while families enjoy their picnics in the sun.

"Jamie?" I squeeze his hand to get his attention.

Don't ask. Don't ask. Don't ask.

"Yeah?" he answers, his eyes watching his toes run through the water.

"Do you ever get attached?"

He looks up, a small groove growing between his brows. "Not usually."

My heart drops, and I give myself a thousand whiplashes for going there. "It's a job, right?"

He sighs. "Usually."

Usually?

When my fingers stiffen in his hand, he continues, "All the women I've been with, they had something they needed healing from. That's what I tell myself when they go home. I'm not there for me." He smiles, but it doesn't quite reach his eyes. "You don't teach a bird to fly to lock it up in a cage."

I nod politely.

"You'll see. When you hook up with your boyfriend in a couple of days, you won't remember any of this. I'm just a transition, Raven."

I push the emotions back down. It's not a conversation I want to have, but maybe Jamie's right. Maybe things will be different when I see Dylan again, now that I'm exorcizing all of my demons. "Maybe."

When the sky above us darkens, he checks his watch and sighs. "We better head back," he says. "It's almost a three-hour trip from here at this time of day."

In the awkward silence, we climb back up until the car's in view. The temperature's dropped, and I'm a little tired. "Will you be all right driving?"

"Of course." He unlocks the car, opens the door, and right before I climb into the passenger seat, he freezes.

"What the fuck?" he yells and crouches by the car. "You gotta be kidding me."

I step outside, my eyes searching for whatever the hell's got his knickers in a twist. And then I see it. The tyre, flat as a pancake.

Shit.

Looks like we're not going anywhere.

Chapter Eleven

J amie swipes his hand over his face a couple of times, deep creases lining his forehead. He runs a palm over the rubber until his fingers find a gash the size of his thumb. He puffs a hard breath as he fiddles with the puncture. "That will need to be replaced."

"Do you have roadside assistance?" My belly twists at the turn of events. The sun's going down, and at this rate, nightfall won't be too far.

He pivots towards me, and a grimace distorts his face. "Baby, I'm a twenty-seven-year-old healthy male. Trust me, I can change a tyre." He marches towards the boot, flips it open, and curses when whatever he's looking for isn't there. "Fucking Hayden."

My feet shuffle closer to him, and I peek over his shoulder. "What did Hayden do?"

He points to the massive empty space under the mat. "My cousin." He grabs a couple of water bottles from the corner of the boot and hands me one. "Used my car last week and didn't put the spare back."

When he leans against the sedan, dark shadows underlining his eyes, then sighs, I snake my arms around his waist and hug him. "It's okay. We'll work it out."

His shoulders drop. "I'm gonna have to make a call."

Ha. There goes your no electronics policy, champ.

He leads me to the passenger side of the car and pushes his seat back until his legs are stretched in front of him.

My jaw drops when he pulls a mobile phone out of the glove box, and it lights up with his name. "What?" My eyes go from him to the device. "You rebel."

He rolls his eyes and scrolls along the screen until he finds Natalie's name. "It's a shit rule anyway. There was no way we were driving six hours without a phone."

The ringing tone blares through the console until Natalie's voice comes through the other end.

"Hey, Jamie, what's up? A bit late for a routine check-in. Everything okay?"

"Hey. I'm not going to be able to report tonight. I've got a flat and no spare."

"Right," she grumbles. "How long do you have left with your client?"

"A day." He avoids looking at me when he answers.

"I'll ring her and see what we can do. We can send a replacement." A rustling of paper comes through the speakers. "Dan is free, or we can give her a partial refund on her package. Not ideal, but I'm guessing you're telling me you can't get back tonight, right?"

"No." He clears his throat. "We're interstate."

There's some grizzling on the line, and for a minute, neither of them speaks. When her tone comes through, it's pitchy, and she's spitting a hundred words per minute. "What do you mean *we*. You better not be implying what I think you're implying."

He glances in my direction, then inhales a deep breath that echoes between us. "I guess I am."

I can see why the phone is the least of his worries.

"You've taken a client outside the hotel, and even worse, you've taken her across the border? Who do you think you are? Her boyfriend?" Natalie's screaming blows my eardrums, and Jamie instantly lowers the volume as she scolds him.

Jamie rotates so he's once again not looking at me when he hisses back, "I don't need a damn lecture from you, Nat. I know what this looks like. I'll bring her back as soon as I get the tyre replaced."

She scoffs. "That's a lawsuit waiting to happen. I don't know what you were thinking."

Neither do I, but my heart swells a little knowing he's breaking the rules for me.

His jaw clenches, his gaze zeroed in on something in the distance. When his chest falls deeper, I grab his hand. Our eyes meet, and he gives me an uncomfortable smile, but laces his fingers with mine.

"Do you need me to book you a hotel?" Natalie's voice lowers, the Aussie Paradise damage-control mode clearly in action.

"Thanks, but no. I'd rather spend the night at the estate, instead of scavenging for a decent room all night."

"Christ, Jamie."

Based on the way she spews the comment, I'm guessing he's breaking another rule.

I just don't know which one it is.

When he's disconnected the call, he shifts until we're facing each other. "I'm sorry you had to hear that."

"I'm guessing you have your own bylaws." I clench my fingers around his. "And we're not quite following them."

He blows a hard breath before he orders an Uber on his phone. "And it's about to get worse."

My eyes scan the massive three-story house in front of us, as the Uber driver manoeuvres around the circular driveway and disappears through the eight-foot electric gates.

God Almighty. What is this place?

White columns showcase an impressive porch that leads to double-glass doors, and when they burst open, Jamie pulls us up the stairs. "Let me introduce you."

An attractive older woman dashes to his side: mid-length dark-brown hair, a loose lilac suit, matching jewellery, and bright lipstick. She meets him halfway. "Jamie! What a surprise."

He gives her a quick hug before he drags me to him. "We were in the area. This is Raven."

If this is a previous client, I'm hitchhiking home.

The woman studies me, a huge grin lighting up her face, before she envelops me in her arms. "Welcome, lovely girl. About time Jamie brought a woman home."

Home?

The chandeliers above our heads guide our way through the mansion, the ten-foot ceilings dwarfing me by size and opulence. We step inside the house, and I scan the photos on the walls until I recognise a very familiar face.

OMG, that's him!

As we stroll through the foyer, Jamie motions to a sofa in one of the living areas. I follow as he chitchats with the woman about some local news. He hands me my cardigan, and we settle on the velour fabric. The woman sinks into an armchair across from us.

"Raven, this is my mother—*Angela*."

My mouth opens, my lips frozen as the resemblance hits me in the face. The striking blue eyes, the straight-edged nose, and the confidence as they lean back against the cushions with similar postures.

I see where he gets his charisma from.

I shuffle forward, butterflies in my chest fluttering as I introduce myself. "So pleased to meet you," I utter. "You have a lovely home."

When Jamie notices the shaking in my fingers, he moves closer until the warmth of his thigh settles me, and within a second, my hands lie still in my lap.

In my defence, it's not like I was briefed before this little *detour*.

"My dear son, as much as I love you, I know you too well to guess this isn't a planned visit." Angela tilts her head in an exaggerated fashion, a relaxed smile stretching her cheeks.

He smiles back. "Planned visits are boring, *Mother Dear*. This is more spontaneous."

She chuckles. "I'll have your room ready. How long are you staying?"

He shakes his head as he extends his feet under the coffee table. "We'll take the second guest room if that's okay."

Her mouth rounds into an O, like he said something hilarious. "The guest quarters?" She grins. "Someone wants privacy."

Heat crawls along my cheeks, my heart rate quickening. I feel like a teenager in the middle of some kinky argument. Jamie's mother definitely isn't coy.

"Raven." Her eyes are kind. "How did you meet my son?"

I freeze as Angela studies me. How the hell do I answer that?

Orgasms-R-Us?

"Hmm." When my feet start tapping on the ground, Jamie comes to my rescue.

"In a Kinder Surprise, Mother. Best prize ever."

She narrows her eyes at him and purses her lips. "That, my dear," she says to me, "is my son guarding his privacy like a rabid dog."

He grins, some unspoken message between them.

"How's work?" She changes the topic.

My stomach is in my throat. If they start discussing my virginity, I'm out of here. Jamie rubs the top of my hand with the pad of his thumb. For some reason, he's oddly cool about the question.

"Good, actually," he answers. "I'm on leave at the moment, but when I go back, I'm taking on a couple of big mergers."

I zap my head towards him, my brain realigning with the fact that outside of being a part-time escort, he has a real job.

"I have a business redesign in Singapore next month, and then two organisational restructures, mainly looking at branding congruence with their products."

A little flicker ignites in my head. I might only be in my second year, but branding and marketing, I know. And after all, showing off a little won't send me to hell. "How strategic is your brand language?"

He cocks an eyebrow. "I'd say very. I *nurture* all four levels of the pyramid equally."

Jamie's mother leans forward. "You're work colleagues. *I knew it.*"

Laughter fills the room, and Jamie and his mother exchange small talk for the next little while.

Then, when her smartwatch chimes, she checks the notification and excuses herself. "I'm afraid I'm late for a Zoom call." She extends her hand towards me. "But I look forward to catching up over breakfast, Raven."

And in a flash, she's gone, leaving Jamie and me alone in the middle of this mansion.

He pulls me to my feet and leads me to a set of double stairs that go on for what feels like kilometres of sky-climbing. "Talk about a change of plans, hey?"

I chuckle. *That's a fucking understatement.*

We climb up, passing a variety of rooms, each as stylish as

the last. When we finally reach the room Jamie claimed for the night, I ask, "Why didn't you want your regular room?"

He pushes the door open before he carries me over the threshold and lays me on the king-size bed.

Slight tickles bud in my lower belly when our eyes meet.

He runs his hands over my thighs and tosses his shoes in a corner of the room. Then, he hovers over me and murmurs, "Because there're three floors between us and my mother, and when you scream my name, I guarantee you that not one soul in town will save you."

Chapter Twelve

I grab Jamie's face with both of my hands and kiss him on the lips. They're soft. Warm. Unguarded. His tongue caresses mine, slowly, like we have all the time in the world.

I guess we do.

Being stranded in the middle of nowhere, in his childhood home, strips what's left of the formal escort. Jamie's depth is lighter here. Genuine. Like we've stumbled into the abyss of his soul.

Something flickers in his gaze, and he studies me as he slowly spreads my legs with his knee. "Just so we're clear, baby. You may have met my mother and now know the deep, dark secrets of my real life, but don't be fooled into thinking I'm going to turn into a choir boy."

I smirk as I crawl higher on the bed, my skirt bundling above my underwear with the friction. "No?"

He shakes his head. "No." His stubble scratches the inside of my thighs as he hums against my skin in a low voice.

I'm instantly flooded with tension, electric niggles that make my insides quiver. Like he knows which buttons to push, he flirts with the hormones building inside me until all I feel is the blood rushing through my core.

He pauses, resting his nose on my flesh, and inhales my scent deep into his lungs. "You're in my house now. You're all mine."

Heat pools in my lower region. I clench my abs as I press my back onto the pillows. "Show me, then."

His pupils darken until they're a midnight blue. They're staring back at me like I'm something to eat, and he's been starved for centuries. His face twitches, and his hands clamp the tops of my legs, right above my knees. "I want to taste you."

The butterflies grow in my belly until they trample my insides like possessed drones. My thighs quiver. I want him too. So fucking badly.

"Where no one has ever tasted you." Wetness seeps through my underwear and he groans in appreciation. His thumb slides up and down the material. "You're drenched already." He slides two fingers behind the cotton, and toys with the seam.

Right as I expect to feel him closer, *need* him closer, deep grooves appear on his face, and he exhales before he says, "Raven, do you con…"

My ankles have his waist pinned between my legs in a millisecond as his thumbs imprint on my thighs from the shock. "You have my consent. Once and for all. To make love to me. To fuck me. Hard or slow, and in every position," I growl as I reach for the top of his head and fist his hair. "I want to feel your tongue on me, Jamie."

His jaw tightens, his pupils dilating to full moons. He swallows thickly, and a corner of his lips curls as he hooks my panties with his pointer finger. "You asked for it." He pulls his shirt above his head and tosses it, then unbuckles his belt. "I'm going to fuck you with my tongue, then with my fingers and my cock until there's no innocence left in you."

There's an intensity in his gaze that both scares and excites me all at once. I whimper when his finger teases my entrance.

"Don't let anyone tell you that you weren't born for this." In one swift motion, he has my underwear ripped off me. He pushes against my thighs until my legs spread wider for him. Then, he braces himself on his elbows so he can appreciate all of my nakedness, his eyes admiring my folds like he's just solved the riddle to an existential question.

"It's perfect." He grazes stray kisses on each side of me, and I tense, my back arched in slow agony.

He blows gently on my lips. Slowly. Appreciatively. Like it's as much for him as it is for me. His breath is warm, and it tickles me *there*. My thighs spread wider on their own, and I lift a knuckle to my mouth, my foreign sounds muffled in my bite.

"There's no point fighting it, Raven. You *are* going to scream for me."

Jesus, Mother of Christ.

I bring my knees up, and quiver when his mouth laps at my lips. "Oh god."

"Wrong name," he says. "Let's see if I can make you say it right." He circles my clit with his tongue. First slowly. Then faster, until he has me squirming under him.

I'm about to explode from the torture, the anticipation, but he doesn't stop. He just keeps going, every atom in my body feeling the burn. Every neuron in my brain firing.

"Jamie," I whimper. My pelvis meets his mouth halfway.

"Hmm?" He pushes his tongue in my slit, as deep as he can, not stopping until I'm bucking beneath him. "You taste amazing."

"I can't handle any more," I cry. My hands search for his head between my legs.

One finger swipes my wetness. "Yes, you can. We're just getting started." His tongue returns to my bud, and it swipes in an up-and-down motion until my body trembles.

I climb until there's nowhere to climb, my insides burning. Like a scorching heat wave in the middle of the desert. My hands fist his hair and I lock my thighs against his cheeks.

"I'm going to put a finger in you," he murmurs against my mound.

His thick finger stretches me until it's buried deep. *I can't hold it.* White lights fill my vision, my lungs ablaze. His finger thrusts in and out as Jamie's tongue emulates a similar dance. My body is tight. Wound up. Pleading for relief. "Please," I beg.

"What's my name, Raven?" A second finger teases me. "Let's see if you can take two, beautiful girl."

The pressure builds, the inside of my vagina dancing to a new tune. "Please, Jamie, please."

"That's better," he hums before he pushes deeper into me, exploring until he says, "There's your G-spot. It's as ready as the rest of you."

His fingers continue their torturous massage, and I writhe on the bed, my moaning growing louder.

"Do you want me to make you come, Raven?"

A thousand stars cloud my vision, and I fear that I might die. The world spins faster, my breathing uncontrolled.

Can you die from coming?

"Make me come, Jamie," I scream his name as I pull his hair like a possessed woman. My legs stiffen, my stomach clenches, and I lose all coherent thoughts as my climax seizes me.

Jamie's mouth devours my clit, his tongue licking my wetness as I come undone, his fingers fucking me in all the right places. I pant as I ride my orgasm, and before I've had time to recover, I'm flipped on my stomach and bent over the mattress.

Jamie pushes my feet apart with his, my arms now spread in a cross. He's right behind me, his hands stroking me from the top of my neck to my ass.

"Open your legs wider for me, baby." His palms stroke me between my thighs, his manhood teasing my entrance.

Excitement buzzes at the unfamiliar. Ass on display, I'm exposed to him. *His*, to play with. As turned on as I am, a small part of me wonders what to expect this time.

"Shit," he says. He leans over until he's rummaged through the bedside drawers and a condom appears.

In a guest bedroom?

It's on in record time. He lines up his cock, right at the base of my slit, sliding it up and down. It glides like it belongs there. Then he lowers himself, his fingers trailing my arms, and murmurs into my ear, "If this hurts, I'll stop, okay?"

My body relaxes with his words. "It won't."

I actually can't know for sure. *But I do.* The tip of his penis pushes past my entrance, filling me. Unlike last time, there's no burning. Just a comfortable stretch, and when he moves, tingles spread through my core as I adjust to his size.

He grips my hips and thrusts hard until his pelvis is ramming into me. With each plunge, his noises grow louder. The intensity rises, and it's not long before I feel a second climax teasing me. My breathing grows shallow. His, erratic. His fingers dig into my skin, like he's trying to get through me, and for a second, I think he might. His thrusts are rough. Focused. Determined.

"Oh god," I whimper against the bed, my body rocking up and down with the motion, pleasure overflowing as electrical currents zap me every time Jamie hits the right spot.

"Come for me again," he growls.

That's all I need for my body to explode around him; stars send me dizzy as I grip onto the sheets and ride the Jamie wave.

He grunts as he slams me harder. Deeper. His legs stiffen against mine, until they feel like concrete. I push against his force, meeting him halfway. It feels fucking amazing.

My body purrs. My mind whistles. And my heart chants.

Then, his hands lock me into place as he lets go of a deep breath and quivers against me. When the thrusts relax, his fingers stroke my back, and he kisses me between my shoulder blades.

"You're perfection, Raven." He flips me over and kisses each of my breasts.

"You're not too bad yourself, lover boy." I trail my fingers on his forearm while I catch my breath. "I'm guessing no pizza delivery here?"

Chapter Thirteen

W hen our bodies have stopped quivering, Jamie pulls himself off me, wraps up the condom, and shrugs into his jeans. "I'll show you the kitchen. There's more food in that pantry than in a 7-Eleven."

I smooth my skirt, then my hair, and slip into my flats. "Good. 'Cause I'm hungry."

More like starving.

Jamie isn't lying. The kitchen is huge. There's fresh food, frozen food, and a thousand cans of everything under the sun. "Who lives here?" I ask.

He purses his lips. "My mother's the constant—well, at least since she got divorced seven years ago. My father, we don't have much to do with him. It's her house. Everyone, from me and my brother to our cousins and family friends, we all take turns crashing here regularly. It's the Kendricks' home base, you could say."

He digs through the fridge until he has a rainbow assortment of ingredients on the bench, and he's prepping something. "I'll make you my specialty. Fried capsicum with savory mince. You'll love it." A frying pan comes out, and he bangs and knocks plates and cutlery, the noise so loud I'm surprised Angela hasn't called the cops.

I eye the staircase, a nail in my mouth.

He glances in my direction. "She won't come down. She's either asleep or working. Check the second room on your right. That's her office."

I tug on my earlobe. "You want me to barge into her office?"

"She won't be in there. Then you'll know, and you can stop freaking out." He leans forward and kisses me. "And if she is, tell her I'm making food."

My brow hurts from being pinched so tightly, but I suppose Jamie's right. If she's in the next room as I'm strolling in her house with no underwear, I'd rather know. "Okay."

I tippy-toe through the open kitchen, then the massive foyer, until I'm standing in front of Angela's office. I peer through the open doors, and gasp when my brain takes in what I'm looking at.

The room is what I expected. Classy, affluent. Of good taste. There's a mahogany desk in the corner, a state-of-the-art laptop that's probably lighter than my watch, and a bookshelf that holds more books than the Brisbane State Library. There're armchairs around a coffee table, flyers and tissues stacked neatly between the seats.

Who visits her to cry?

That's not just an office. Once I've made sure that Angela isn't inside, I step into the sanctuary, and freeze when my eyes catch the art hanging on the wall.

A couple making love, their limbs intertwined as they share an intimate moment. My eyes look away, my heart beating like I've been caught prying.

I run a finger along the bookshelves, my mind processing each title, every new one more specific than the last.

The Elusive Orgasm

The Real Guide to Life as a Couple
Mating in Captivity

I narrow my eyes and zone in on the statues in the glass cabinet. They're all naked, and they're either having sex or masturbating. I lurch away.

What have I walked into?

My back hits a wall, and I pivot until I'm facing a larger table—on top of it, sex toys galore. Fingers shaking, I pick up a pink contraption, still in its original packaging, and bring it closer to my face.

What the hell is this? All of it?

A shadow across the office startles me, and I almost drop the toy. I gasp and pivot. Jamie's leaning against the door frame, his arms crossed. He's biting his bottom lip, his eyes going around the room like he's seeing it for the first time.

"Someone's been redecorating." He whistles as he crosses the distance between us.

My stomach plummets. "I'm sorry... I didn't mean to."

He drops a kiss on my forehead. "Get out of your head." Jamie picks up one of the other toys, some long cylinder with various textures inside it, then clamps it shut. "And upgrading her resources."

Confusion dances inside my head, and I battle the alternatives fighting in my mind. I don't know what scares me the most: the idea that my liver will be sold on the black market, or that I'm about to be turned into a sex slave.

"What's all this?" I murmur and point to the art, the books, the brochures, and the various sex toys on display.

"That reminds me." He marches to a cabinet and pulls the double doors open. A bunch of underwear, from thongs to cotton and lace, of all shapes and sizes and still with tags, cascades out. He turns towards me and quips, "What are we in the mood for today?"

My eyes grow wide.

I'm not wearing his mother's underwear.

He watches the colour drain from my face and laughs. "They're samples. She gets them sent from sponsors. Don't be coy. Pick one."

I shuffle until I'm by his side and nip the first one that looks about my size. A purple cotton brief covers my private parts underneath my skirt in less than a second. I'm relieved, but also curious. Jamie doesn't seem concerned.

"What does she do for a job?"

At this rate, anything but a human trafficker would be an upgrade.

"She's a sexologist." He points to multiple frames on the wall behind the desk.

I tilt my head, my eyes squinting. I march to all the degrees, awards, and certificates, and I freeze.

Dr Angela Kendrick—Sexologist—PhD.

A string of magazine covers, journal articles, and various photos of Jamie's mother on radio shows—hell, there's even one with Oprah—slap me in the face.

Holy cow. That's the *Dr Angela Kendrick.*

Award winning author of best-sellers on human sexuality. Radio host on all matters of female orgasms. Australia's best couple therapist for the last five years in a row.

And I'm wearing her underwear.

Jamie's laugh snaps me out of my daze. "I can't tell if you're shell-shocked or starstruck."

"Both?" I utter.

Visions of the last two days fill my mind. There's a reason Jamie knows so much about sex and women. He presses all the right buttons, and he shares sexual values that go beyond the role of an escort.

"Let's sit down." He guides me to what I'm guessing is the counselling area, and I crumple on one of the chairs.

I take deep breaths until the surprise has vaporised out of my pores. "So, she's your mum?"

"She's my mum."

"How many sex talks did you get growing up?"

He chuckles. "I've stopped counting. She caught me masturbating at fifteen and scolded me for holding myself too tight, death grip and all."

My mind buzzes. "Death grip?"

"Holding your dick too tight can lead to erectile dysfunction with vaginal intercourse later..."

Oh, shit.

I plug my ears with the tip of my fingers and cut him off. "Okay. Okay. Please stop talking." I blow a hard breath and shake my hands until I'm *pent-up energy* free.

Next to me, Jamie crosses his legs. He leans back against his chair and scans the office, a fat smile stretching his lips. "I've spent so much time in this room. Learning all there was to learn about the female anatomy, their arousal patterns, and how gorgeous an empowered woman can be."

"So, you're basically a sex god on steroids."

"Hey, I'll take the compliment."

"Someone's sexcapades are going to his head." I laugh and toss the box of tissues at him.

He catches it mid-flight. "Seriously though. It's not just about the sex."

Jamie pauses, like there's plenty he's not saying. It fuels my need to understand him. His motives. His fears. His dreams. The man must have a reason for the double life.

"Why do you do the escort thing, then? Why not just have Tinder dates like the rest of the world."

He sighs. "Because these women I'm seeing, they're picked for a reason. They've all gone through shit one way or another." He gives me a dampened smile. "They all deserve to be held through their pain. There's something about the way intimacy heals the soul."

It all makes sense now.

"Why?"

There's a twinkle in his eye. It's both a mixture of hope and sadness.

"Because one day, I'll have a woman by my side. She'll be loved in every fucking possible way, for the rest of her life. I'll hold her when she cries, protect her when she's afraid, and fuck her when she's turned on. But never, ever, will she need to hide from me when she's vulnerable."

The energy in the room shifts. It crackles with tension.

Then, just as I was about to speak, Jamie offers me his hand to guide me back to the kitchen. "That's what I wish for you and Dylan."

Chapter Fourteen

S unrays kiss my face through the window. They wake me up from my drowsy state. Palm raised to my eyes, I squint as the room materialises around me.

Pillows and blankets lie on the floor, the sheet over me crinkled from last night's sexy cuddle therapy. I stretch and yawn before pushing myself upright on the bed.

The empty bed.

The spot where Jamie slept last night's still warm. I run my fingers around the invisible shadow, tinges of disappointment clouding me when he's nowhere in sight. Memories of curling into his arms tug at my heartstrings, and I smile to myself when my body remembers the comforting presence. It's something I could get used to.

I roll over until my nose is inhaling his pillow, and I'm drunk on the cocktail of musk, sweat, and the scent of lovemaking lingering around the bedroom. I sigh at the bittersweet awakening.

How will I go back to real life tomorrow?

My hips swing to the side of the bed, my toes touching the

ground, and right before I'm about to jump to my feet, my eyes catch a note folded upright on the bedside table.

Good morning beautiful,

There're clothes and a fresh towel in the en suite. When you're ready, come down. You're all that's missing for breakfast.

The summer dress fits me perfectly, and I don't dare ask where it came from. Based on how it barely covers my thighs, I'm guessing it's not Angela's.

My feet slide over every step, my belly tight, as I make my way down the three flights of stairs that lead to the kitchen. Jamie's voice resonates through the high ceilings. It's followed by glass clinking, and his mother adding to their conversation.

Curiosity jabs me. Their voices grow louder, and I pause when I land on the threshold, my ears prickling when I hear my name.

"I didn't know you were dating?"

My breath hitches. The corner of the wall digs into my shoulders, but I press deeper into it until the sound of Jamie's voice vibrates through the plasterboard.

"It's complicated."

"Then, uncomplicate it. How hard can it be?" There's liquid being poured and spoons stirring against ceramic. Jamie remains silent while Angela sips on something. Then she adds, "She's young."

He sighs. "I know."

"But you don't care." A small chuckle escapes her, followed by more sipping.

"No." More clunking. "I don't. But she's not mine to keep."

There's a stretch of silence, like Angela's processing his comment. My shoulder goes numb against the staircase, and I'm pretty sure my shape's now permanently engraved in the concrete.

"She's not yours or anyone's *to keep*, Jamie. If I've taught you anything in the last three decades, it's that women are not objects. She belongs to herself first and foremost. Once she figures this out, the rest will fall into place. Just have a bit more trust in the universe, son."

A chair scrapes against the tiles, and I freeze, my heart dropping to my stomach. Snooping isn't something I'd be proud to be caught doing. Even when what he's saying makes no sense.

She's not mine to keep.

"I'm going to go and find her, okay?" Jamie's tone is neutral.

A deep breath steadies me, and right as Jamie turns the corner, I step out of the shadows and almost run into him.

"Hey, you," he says before he pulls me by the waist against him. His arm locks me into place, and he presses a kiss to my forehead. "Did you sleep well?"

I palm his chest. "How could I not?"

We pivot towards the dining room, and by the time Jamie and I reach the glass table, Angela is standing, arms open, a welcoming grin on her face.

"I hope you're hungry." She sweeps a hand over the feast.

My mouth drops open as I process the variety of foods she's put out for us. Croissants. Waffles. Fruits. Yoghurt. Cereals. Bacon. Eggs. Hashbrowns. There're even two types of juice, and fresh coffee's brewing.

I've had all-you-can-eat buffets with less food than that.

"Wow, Angela, thank you. I didn't expect this." My stomach braces for a tantrum, my eyes watering at my choices.

Jamie pulls a chair by what I assume is his. I slide into it, and when Angela motions for me to dig in, I grab a yoghurt and some fruit and pass the plate to her.

"Any plans for today, Jamie?" Angela asks, before a forkful of waffle lands in her mouth. It's not even nine, and she's dressed like she's the epitome of professionalism, in a pair of tight pants and a matching blouse.

It contrasts with the dark sweatpants Jamie's wearing with no shoes. Though I'm not complaining. There's something hot about the way his waistband sits right below his hip bones. I look away when he catches me checking him out, and pretend I don't notice the beam stretching his lips.

"We'll have the car back by four," he answers her. "So, until then, I might show Raven around the estate."

He loads his plate with bacon and eggs and pours the three of us some juice. Light conversation resumes, Jamie and his mother taking turns at teasing each other. They include me in their banter, and my heart swells at how easy it is to blend in with them.

Everything's easy when he's around.

Hugs. Chat. Sex. Even talking about my darkness doesn't seem so daunting anymore.

He's not yours to keep.

I swallow the heartbeat pounding in my throat, and slam away the thoughts that midnight's about to strike.

No prince will search for this Cinderella's glass slipper.

Though it shouldn't surprise me, the dishes are dealt with by staff as soon as Angela leaves to start her counselling sessions for the day.

With six hours to spare before we can drive back to Brisbane, Jamie takes my hand and guides me to the back patio. We stand on a balcony, my hands grabbing on the banister, and I gasp.

"What would you like to do today?" he asks, like we've not stepped in on some *Narnia* replica set.

My eyes scan the view, my shoulders dropping with every new visual. This place is stunning.

Below us, the inground pool sparkles, the sea of blue undulating softly as water streams between rock walls. It's almost as gorgeous as the kilometres of landscape that seem to go on and on, beyond the immediate walls of the estate.

"What's over there?" I point to what looks like a gate leading to some woods.

Jamie stands closer to me, his arms around my waist, his mouth nestled in the crook of my neck. "Tell me," he murmurs against my skin. "Have you ever been on a quad?"

My hand snakes up the back of his neck, and I don't have to turn around to know he's smiling. My Aussie hunk is up to something. "On Tangalooma Island, once."

"Would you like me to show you what's over there?"

I turn until my eyes meet his. "I'd love that."

He kisses me, then playfully smacks me on the butt. "All right. We're gonna need to change. I'll find you some clothes."

This house is like a magician's hat. Everything comes out of it, and I have no idea how the trick works. Within ten minutes, I'm dressed in jeans and a t-shirt, and my feet are wearing runners. It's not as glamourous, but to be honest, it's probably the most comfortable I've felt in the last few days.

When Jamie comes out of the bathroom, he's dressed in cargo pants and a black V. I almost faint at how fucking melting hot he is. He's complete eye candy. My tongue runs over my bottom lip, and he smirks.

He so knows.

Heat creeps up my neck, and I pray to God I'm not crimson. He saunters towards me, his eyes narrowed, and teases, "See something you like?"

I shake my head. "Nope. You're old and decrepit. It's gross."

He laughs, grabs my hand, and says, "We'll see how old I am when I have you alone in the woods."

What he calls a shed is bigger than my flat. Inside, there're four different quads, all lined up like racing monsters. He hands me a helmet and pulls one of the machines into the middle of the building.

"Okay, baby. This is important." He pats the seat until I'm sitting on it. "You don't want to be pinned under one of those, so listen up."

We go through every lever, handle, and part, until I could rebuild the Suzuki LT-Z50 in my sleep. There's a line between Jamie's brow as he repeats his instructions multiple times. When he's done, he fastens the helmet on my head, securing the clip under my chin, and checks it twice before he puts his own on.

"I'll lead, okay? Just follow me." His hand squeezes my clenched fist on the lever, and he disappears behind me until his engine is revving. The red machine takes over mine, and drawing a deep breath, I release my clutch and the quad moves forward.

All the way to the gate, Jamie glances over his shoulder, making sure I'm right behind him. He relaxes once we plunge into the woodland, and I can see why.

There're hundreds of trees that shade us from the rest of the world, light sunrays chasing us as we climb higher. Then, as we reach a clearance, an open space with deep track marks in the ground, Jamie grins in my direction and pushes on his accelerator until he's way ahead of me.

He's in his element.

Slight electricity buzzes through me, the adrenaline pumping in my blood as I mirror him. I let my bike catch up to his. If he thinks I'm going to lag behind him, he's got another thing coming.

I crush the lever as hard as I can, the motor shrieking as my speed doubles in record time. It takes about 0.001 seconds before I've caught up to Jamie and overtake him in my stride.

"See you later, lover boy," I yell as I pass him.

His eyes are wide.

"Fuck." Shock erupts from him in the distance, right before the sound of his engine roars through the paddock.

I reach the top of the meadow first, and slowly press on my brakes. Jamie pauses next to me. We exchange a glance, and when he registers the hitch in my breath, his face brightens. The loose lock on his forehead gives him a carefree look that's emphasised by the competitive glare he throws my way.

"Someone's being a naughty girl." He dismounts his bike and places his helmet at the back. He marches next to me and offers me his hand until I'm standing by his side.

"That is so beautiful," I mumble. There are no words to describe what lies before our eyes. I can see why he looks like a child on Christmas morning.

The view is out of this world.

An old oak tree overlooks never-ending hills, light leaves surrounding its skirt. Wildflowers of all colours fill the large space. Purple, pink, white, and little yellow blooms, each as perfect as the other, hide among soft greenery, the fresh scent of lemongrass lulling all my senses.

Jamie pulls me forward until we're walking through a cloud of sunshine, our feet gliding across the meadow. Then, right as we hit a glistening stream, he picks me up into his arms, and lifts me over the trickle.

An intimate comfort stirs my core, my soul relishing the incredible peace I feel against him. I slide my arms around his neck, my head cradling his chest until he puts me down by a large cluster of boulders.

"Here we are, beautiful girl," he says, as he pushes a strand of hair behind my ear.

I sigh. "I've never seen anything like it."

"Wait till you see what else I have for you." Jamie's thighs tense as he leaps from one stone to another. Hands in his pockets, he stands tall when he reaches the top of the rock wall. Then, he leans over and surveys whatever's on the other side. "Yesss!" he shouts.

He's back down before a second has lapsed, and I still have no clue as to what has him so excited. "Come on." He bends and pulls me up by both of my hands, not budging an inch when all my weight transfers onto him. His forearms twitch, every muscle in him rippling under his perfect skin.

"Where are we going?" I shout, as I'm being dragged behind him to the top of our mini mountain.

"You'll see. It's the best part."

Chapter Fifteen

My legs burn as I leap over the rocks, my strides shorter than Jamie's. He's flying through the obstacles like he knows the shape of every stone, the placement of every step, and the way the mountain breathes as we climb to the other side.

When we reach the top, I'm breathless, but before I have time to embrace the view, Jamie locks me against his hip.

I freeze.

Holy Mother of God.

We're standing above a magnificent waterfall, and it's probably one of Australia's most hidden gems. Though I've been born and bred in Queensland, I've yet to see something as powerful as this.

It's breathtaking.

A cascade vibrates right under our feet. It pools below in a sea of deep, aqua water in the middle of our own utopia.

There's not one soul in sight. The only sounds around us are from the bright-coloured Lorikeets chirping between the native trees. The smell of sweet honey tickles my nostrils, and it takes me about a minute of trailing the birds to work out we're surrounded by rare fauna.

Jamie shifts to his left until he's picked a flower from a Grevillea bush in one swift move. He gently brings the fuchsia bud to my nose, exhilaration glistening in his eyes. "That's what you can smell. The indigenous elders call them bush lollies."

A deep breath has me inhaling the sweet nectar from his hand. It smells beautiful. I wrap my fingers around his wrist and close my eyes as I fight the senses battling in my psyche.

I wonder how many girls he's brought up here as he was growing up.

Is he enjoying this as much as I am?

Is this all truly a professional act?

My heart taunts me with emotions I shouldn't feel for him, and my throat tightens when he pulls me into a hug.

Anyone in a place like this would feel sentimental. Don't let that make you assume things that aren't there, Raven.

"I've been here a thousand times," he murmurs against the top of my head. "But it's different today."

I give him a bittersweet smile before I turn towards the view. "Don't tell me this is part of the estate."

He chuckles. "Okay, I won't."

My head jerks towards him. "Are you serious? For real?"

A kiss lands on my forehead. "Uh-huh. Seven generations, and a truckload of memories." He points to a man-made landing a couple of metres below us, to our right. "And there, is where we'll create a new one."

My eyes narrow, my head tilting as I give him a puzzled look. Then I peek down, and my stomach drops. *We're bloody freaking high above ground.*

There's at least a ten-metre drop encased in natural embankment, and though it's pristine, the rock pool at the bottom looks like it could fit in a teacup.

The height taunts me as I follow him down the path laid out in front of us. When we reach the lower plateau, I breathe a little easier, my shoulders relaxing, until Jamie tosses his runners to the side and pulls his shirt over his head.

"Let's see if I'm still old." He laughs as he unbuckles his cargos. They drop to the ground before they're tossed in a pile by his feet.

Panic fills me, a dizzy spell shaking my ability to ask him what the hell he's doing. All I can do is stare, frozen, and pray to God that denial sets in fast.

Because there's no universe where I want to hear what he's suggesting.

My mouth goes dry, my eyes darting between him and the open space—or rather, the cliff of death he's dangerously flirting with.

In front of me, Jamie stands in his boxers, his taut body pumped like he's bracing for a marathon. He leans over the edge and beams. "I was worried the water would be low. But it's perfect." Then, he turns towards me. "Why are you still dressed?"

I blink, the question not registering. If he's implying what I think he is, he's out of his freaking mind.

I step away until my back hits the wall.

No way. No fucking way.

He nods, his pupils dilated like he's birthing the sun, his lips showing perfect white teeth through the broadest grin of the century.

"You're crazy, Jamie Kendrick, if you think you're coming near me right now."

A laugh explodes from his chest, his eyes sparkling at the challenge. He takes a step towards me, until I'm cornered between two rocks. "Baby... Last time I checked, you weren't afraid of a little wetness, were you?" His hands fiddle with the buttons of my jeans.

"No. No way. I can't."

"I'll tell you what. Why don't we get you a little less…" He twirls a finger in the air as he points at my clothes. "…dressed, so you can enjoy the sunshine?"

My eyes narrow to slits. "Do you think I was born yesterday?"

His grin grows, though I didn't think it possible. "Strip for me."

"Get lost." I bite the inside of my mouth to stop my lips from curling.

I lose that battle when he gets on his knees and opens my jeans. Slowly. With both hands. His thumbs hook around the belt loops and slide them down until his face is resting on my lower belly. He presses a kiss right above the lace of my underwear. Hot air fills my lungs, my blood pumping harder as his palms pull me closer to him. Nibbles trail from my stomach to the top of my thighs.

I exhale, my fingers running through his hair. I swear it's grown longer in just a few days.

"Do you remember when you didn't think I could make you feel good?" His voice is muffled against my skin.

My jeans fall to my ankles. I step outside the material, one foot at a time, and pretend I don't see my pants land on top of his clothes.

"Hmm." My eyes close when he pulls my underwear to the side. My fingers grip his hair. Tight. A groan leaves his throat when I pull it, and the sound sends magical decibels through my core, my clit vibrating ever so slightly.

His tongue flicks my bud, the sucking noises drowning out the internal monologue screaming between my ears, reminding me that we're still standing on top of a cliff. Warmth fills me. It cyclones in my lower region until it gushes through me. My legs threaten to buckle.

He snakes his forearm around my ass until I'm not going

anywhere. Then, right as he steadies me, he says, "Take the shirt off."

"No."

His tongue circles my clit faster, his arm pinning me against his face. He glances up. "Yes."

God Almighty.

I almost come on the spot as my eyes stare into his. His pupils are dark. Confident. There's a charismatic aura to his demand. Like there's no doubt in his mind I'll comply and that I'll love every minute of it.

Jamie's not asking me. *He's telling me.*

Ordering me.

And I fucking love it.

The shirt slips easily off my shoulders, and I toss it with the rest. With his palms, Jamie spreads the top of my thighs until his whole mouth is eating my centre like I'm the most refined dessert he's ever had. My dew drips into his mouth, and he drinks it as if I make it for him.

This should be disgusting. Revolting. *Shameful.*

But it's not. It's empowering, mind-blowing, incredibly hot, and I want nothing more than to come in his mouth as I watch him swallow my orgasm.

Electricity pinches me, and a frenzy builds with every stroke of his tongue. I clamp my legs, stiffening, the addictive wave brewing in my pelvis like a Queensland storm. I gasp when he bites my clit and buries a thick finger between my folds.

Intoxicated by desire, I whimper, my pelvis meeting him halfway, until I'm higher than this mountain.

"Jamie," I whisper, as he curls his finger, deep thrusts sending spasms of pleasure through my whole body. "Oh god." I brace myself on his shoulders with both of my hands as stars flash before my eyes, and I ride my climax against his lips.

My body convulses. It shivers as my legs give way to my

weight, but before I crash against the hard rocks, Jamie's on his feet, his chest against mine.

Warm. Solid. Safe.

A god in the shell of a mortal.

I lean against him and wrap my arms around his torso. His heart beats fast against my ear, my blood still rushing from his sweet torture. Speechless, I cuddle him as he strokes my back. There's nothing that doesn't feel good with this man.

"Relax against me, Raven."

I chuckle and nuzzle my nose right above his collarbone. "How can I not be relaxed after that, lover boy?"

Behind my back, his forearms pin me against him. It's so tight it almost hurts, but when he kisses me, I ignore it.

"Exactly," he whispers in my ear.

Our eyes meet. His, jet-black. By the time I decode the grin on his face, and my brain has caught up, it's too late.

Eyes transfixed in stupor, my mouth opens, but I make no sound. I'm frozen in Jamie's arms, my nails clawing at his back. Blood drains from my veins until my throat has dried to sandpaper, and fear is etched in every crease on my face. My stomach contracts into a tight ball, my heart hammering through the whole estate.

The last thing I feel is cold wind blowing against my skin, as Jamie falls backwards over the edge of the cliff.

With me in his arms.

Chapter Sixteen

As we freefall through the air, crippling fear paralyses me until all of my limbs feel foreign. Numb. Eyes pressed shut, I wrap myself around Jamie, my mouth opened in a silent scream.

In my mind, the piercing shriek travels through space, rips open every portal, and pulverises every planet along the way.

But it dies when I force my eyes open, the world suddenly reborn.

I gasp.

Everything around us is in motion. It flies past us at a speed beyond comprehension, as do sounds and lights. And all sensations. I can feel the atoms stroking my pores, and the nerve endings regenerating in my spine. There's a new freedom that laces through my mind, until all my fear, panic, and suffering have cowered to the new me.

I'm invincible. Unstoppable. Hungry for more.

Gravity fuels my thirst, and I surrender to its will.

I'm falling. Yet, I'll be fine. I just know it.

Tucked inside Jamie's chest, I laugh. And as soon as I do,

Jamie screams mid-air, a glorious war call that announces our victory. Mine follows.

It's exhilarating.

Right as the water looms, Jamie slides his palm to the back of my neck. I'm pinned against him as he breaks our fall.

He hits the water before me, feet first. I'm milliseconds behind him.

The impact takes my breath away, and I will my lungs to pause as we dive underwater. Jamie's grip loosens, and instead, his fingers find mine. Even in the eye of a waterfall, my body pumping with crippling adrenaline, his smile has me melting as he pulls us to the surface.

A deep breath fills my chest when we emerge, and a thousand megawatts of tingling sensations prickle under my skin as I latch onto him.

"Oh my god!" My arms spring to life, my legs kicking in the rock pool, as I pash him like never before. "We could have died!"

He returns the kiss ten-fold as he propels me out of the water in his arms. My legs curl around his waist as he lowers me again.

"I'd never let you die." He swipes the hair away from my eyes and grabs my face with both hands. "But if you tell me that this wasn't the biggest fucking turn-on of your life, I'm calling you a liar."

My heart gallops in my chest and a couple of deep breaths steady me. I shake my head, and laugh, not quite ready to admit he's bloody right.

This was out of this world.

We swim and cuddle in Jamie's hidden paradise for what seems like an eternity. When goosebumps crawl along my body, he motions for us to get out, and he leads me through a different path to find our clothes. Thank God there's no climbing this time.

Still damp, we slide into our outfits and settle against the concrete wall behind us. I smile at my free toes as they bake in the afternoon sun.

"Thank you for bringing me here," I say.

"You're most welcome," he answers. "I've had a real nice time."

A perfect time.

"In my world, places like these only exist in our dreams."

"That's why we need to create our own. Now that you know they're real, I want you to chase them."

"You make it sound easy." I sigh. "But I'll try."

His tone intensifies. "No, you're not gonna try. You're gonna kick ass. You're going to get everything you didn't think you could, and you'll do it in your sleep. And you know why?" His eyes pierce mine. "Because that's who you are. That's who you were a week ago, even before me. You just didn't know it yet."

I swallow hard, his words dancing in my mind.

That's who I am.

"But now that you do know." A new energy thunders through him as he continues, "My beautiful Raven is going to be successful in every area she's dreamed of. You'll run marketing campaigns for the best of the biggest. You'll marry the hottest stud in town and have the perfect 2.2 children and a house your neighbours will envy." His voice softens. "And when he makes love to you at night, you'll feel every part of his touch. You'll lean into his soul as you share yours with him, loving yourself as much as you love him."

There's a knot in my throat that chokes me, and though I try to speak, words don't form. All I hear is Jamie's heartfelt wish for me, and it kills me that he won't be there to see it.

Silence stretches around us. The unspoken cackling at me.

As if he senses it, Jamie checks the time on his phone and sighs. "The car's back. We should get going."

My fingers trace imaginary lines on my jeans, and I don't look at him when I nod.

Breaking the awkward stillness, Jamie continues, "What exciting plans do you have for the rest of the week?"

I chew the inside of my lips until the taste of metal stings my tongue.

The end of term party on the Gold Coast is where I'm supposed to meet Dylan, Jess, and a bunch of others tonight. But right now, my brain can't comprehend a return to real life.

"Hmm, I'm supposed to meet up with friends." I avoid Jamie's gaze as I stumble over the words, despite knowing he's already aware of my plans.

"It's okay to say you're meeting your boyfriend."

There's a softness in his tone that does nothing but rile me up. I don't want his sympathy. I don't want his handshake as we part ways. What I really want is... *this*. No more, no less.

My Jamie in all his glory. Hot. Smart. *Caring.*

If only this weren't a job.

"It all feels a bit..." I clear my throat. "Surreal. I don't know how to pretend this never happened."

He takes my hand and pulls it to his lap. "Baby, you never have to pretend this wasn't real. It's as real as this sunset." He points to the beautiful purple and orange dusk. "But what this was... what it is... is a transition, Raven. Something to show you how strong you are, how fucking awesome you are, and all that you can achieve moving forward."

More tears well in my eyes, and I swallow a sob. His fingers cling to mine harder.

"It's easy for you. You've probably done this a hundred times before," I nip, and instantly regret it when he pales, his jaw clenched.

"What do you want me to say, Raven? Yes, I've fucked a lot of women. All of whom I've respected through the whole ordeal. I'm not sorry for giving them some hope and a break from their shitty lives. God, that's all I wanted for you."

You're just one of many.

A ragged breath punctures my lungs as visions of Jamie making love to these women drill through my brain. Stroking them. Kissing them. Reminding them how special they are.

What did you think? That you were different?

I shake my head at my stupidity, pain slicing through me like an ice pick chipping at my heart. "I'm sorry."

He lowers himself until our eyes are levelled. "Don't you fucking apologise. You've done nothing wrong. You're filled with hormones—post-trauma healing." He gives me a tender smile that doesn't quite reach his eyes. "Lust. And all this will settle as soon as you're in Dylan's arms. That's why you did all of this, remember?"

Last week seems like a distant memory now.

My walls crumble around me, the ticktock indicating that my time is up blaring in my eardrums. The truth is deafening. "How am I supposed to do *this* with someone else?"

His fingers stroke my hair, shaping each lock into place like he's trying to memorise them. And then it hits me.

After today, I'll never see him again.

A whimper shakes me as I fight to rein in my emotions.

I slip my arms around him, my face hiding in the crook of his neck. "I'm sorry," I cry. "I'm sorry. I just need a minute."

He closes the distance between us, and in one swift move has me cradled in his lap. His arms envelop me, shielding me from my pain, as our eyes meet.

There's angst lining his features, but at the same time, there's resignation there too.

He's at peace with it.

"Shhh," he murmurs in my ear. His hand cups my face,

and he gives me a tender kiss. It's soft. Unhurried. "I promise it won't hurt tomorrow."

I draw a breath. "It's the way it has to be, isn't it?"

"Yes."

My forehead leans against his chest, and it lingers there in silence, until I've swallowed the new sobs threatening to spill. My fingers fist his shirt, my heart bleeding as my mind counts the hours left in my package.

A measly couple of hours till he's in someone else's arms.

"I didn't think it would be this hard, but I'm glad it was you." My voice breaks against his chest, my fists clutching onto him even more.

Even if temporary.

He swallows thickly, his chest rising as he takes a deep breath. I expect him to answer, but he doesn't. Instead, he pushes me back until his eyes stare into mine, and he's lifting my chin with the tip of his fingers.

"What we shared was amazing, and I'm fucking lucky that you chose me to be with you." He pauses until the tremor in his voice dies down. "But what kind of man would I be if I derailed you from your life, your boyfriend, before you've had time to experience it? While you're still in this lust spell?"

"Ethics 101, right?" An awkward chuckle falls between us.

He nods. "Something like that."

"Will I ever see you again?"

His Adam's apple bobs up and down, his eyes glistening. "No, Raven. This is goodbye."

Chapter Seventeen

M y seat belt clicks into the buckle, right as Jamie's Audi passes the threshold of the estate. Behind us, the black metallic gates clunk as they close. I glance in my side-view mirror, my lip wobbling when Angela's waving silhouette diminishes into the background.

Jamie turns the radio on, a couple of hosts arguing over whether paperbacks or e-books are the reading of the future emits through the speakers. Their mumbling fades to white noise in the quiet car ride.

"Are you cold?" Jamie fiddles with the aircon buttons until the engine purrs louder.

"A little."

Truth be told, I'm freezing. It's a miracle I still have my toes. Between the late swim, the limited clothing, and the emotional tsunami that took over me earlier, there's not much left of me.

I'm beat.

The heater blows on full blast, and I extend my hands until they rest right above the vents. The warmth soothes the looming hyperthermia, and I exhale, thankful for the small blessing.

Next to me, Jamie offers his arm in an open hug. "Full-body heat over here."

There's no kink twinkling in his eyes. No sexy time, and definitely no hidden agenda. What I see instead, etched in the line between his brow, is concern.

He sends a comforting smile my way, like he couldn't think of anything more natural. And yet, it feels so *wrong*.

"I'm okay, thank you." Cuddling against him would completely warm me inside out, but it would also make the clean break my brain has finally accepted much harder.

His smile shrinks just a little, and he brings his arm back in until both of his hands rest on the steering wheel. When the silence stretches, he turns the volume up until the car fills with radio hits. I lean against the window, my head jouncing with every bump on the road, until sleep breaks in like a quiet thief.

It feels like we've been driving forever when a melodic tune chimes through the console. It rings and rings, until finally it stops.

Then, Jamie's voice echoes through the loudspeaker, and it takes me about ten seconds to work out who's on the other end of that call.

I shuffle on the leather seat, my butt numb, and let my pupils adjust to the darkness. I must have been asleep for a while, because the midnight sky is all around us when I finally sit upright.

"Hey, Nat." Jamie's voice is thin. Like he's over this day just as much as I am.

Dark circles taint the space under his eyes, and there're lines across his forehead I hadn't noticed until now. He swipes his face as he waits for Natalie to answer.

A tinge of guilt spreads through me. It hadn't occurred to me that this part of the *work* could be taxing on him too.

"Touching base, seeing how you're doing for time. Seems like the apartment hasn't been checked out. Everything okay?"

"Yep." He clears his throat. "I'm about fifteen minutes out, I'd say. Just passed the Springwood exit."

"Good. I wanted to make sure you're okay with your usual schedule for the next week or so."

"I'm listening." His tone's business-like. There's an edge to it, but I can't decipher whether he's relieved, upset, or excited.

"I've got you two intros for tomorrow. One's a girl with a disability, and the other's a bored housewife. Happy for me to book?"

Sinking into my seat, I take a deep breath and settle my heart rate.

Breath in. Breath out.

The concrete wakeup call stings more than I imagined. It smacks me in the head like a boxer in the prime of his life. This is really it.

Jamie glances my way, his lips flat when his eyes meet mine.

Yes, I'm still here, champ.

"That's fine," he adds. "You know the drill."

She inhales loudly, background noises coming through the speaker. "Yeah. Yeah. You'll meet them, but no promises. I know," she says, like she's done this a thousand times.

She probably has.

"How did it end with young Raven?"

Jamie blows a hard breath, his chest rising as he answers, "She's right here. We were delayed."

"What?" she screeches into the receiver. "Her package expired half a day ago!" She takes a second to regroup, then she adds, "I'm so sorry, Raven. Can I please apologise for the inconvenience and change of plans this weekend? This has never happened before. It's highly unprofessional on our part."

I shrug—*as if she can see me.* I don't even care anymore. I just want to go home. "That's fine. These things happen. No one died."

My heart catapults into my throat, the memories of our cliff dive taunting me. Just a couple of hours ago, I lay in Jamie's arms as he protected me from the world.

Now, he's getting ready to do it again.

With someone else.

"We'd like to offer you a one-night package, free of charge, as a gesture of good will and to make up for the time wasted in transit. Daniel would love to meet with you. How does next weekend sound?"

Jamie's hands tighten against the steering wheel, his knuckles white. Jaw clenched. His gaze is fixed on the road. He doesn't even blink.

"Huh, thanks. Can I get back to you later?" I puff out, my fortitude testing me. While I appreciate her efforts, I'm in no rush to repeat this high-voltage, sub-drop experience. Right now, I'm just trying to manage the end of this day in one piece, and it's looking grimmer by the second. Add in the idea that I have to show my face at Jess's end of term party tonight, and I'm considering jumping off that cliff voluntarily.

"Of course, you can. I promise we'll make it up to you."

"Nat, we're pulling in, so we're gonna get going." Jamie interrupts her as the Audi parks in his bay.

"Don't forget tomorrow's assignments." She rushes through her last-minute instructions.

Right before the line goes dead, he deadpans, "Looking forward to it."

The trip up the elevator is as chilly as a Tasmanian holiday. Jamie stands tall, tense, until we're inside the room and packing our suitcases. I dig into my bag and rummage in the

side pocket until I've retrieved my phone. A thousand notifications flash as the device lights up.

Christ Almighty.

Seven messages from Dylan. Love, hearts and kisses, and a
promise for an amazing night tonight. Brain-fogged, I don't
even want to know what that means in his language, and I
send a quick reply.

When twenty notifications from Jess fill my screen, I take
the hint and click on her name.

**Change of plans, babe. Tonight. The Met. Waiting
for your glamourous ass to turn up. And don't even
think about bailing. I know where you live.**

Jesus Christ. As if a party wasn't bad enough, I'm now
summoned to one of the busiest nightclubs in Brisbane City.
While no part of me wants to drag my ass to the drunken play-
ground, if I'm being honest, I'd rather not be alone tonight.

Yep. Give me an hour. With bells and whistles.

Clothes fly in and out of my bag until an emerald cocktail
dress is lined up on the bed. I pull out black shiny heels and
my makeup bag.

If I have to go, I might as well go out with a bang.

A quick shower later, and with Jamie nowhere in the
vicinity, I'm standing in front of a full-length mirror, my body
hugged by the stretchy material. My hair cascades down my
back as I narrow my smoky eyes at the Raven I'm meeting for
the first time.

My lips curl into half-moons as I discover the phoenix in
front of me. Foreign, but familiar, it's a different woman who
stares back at me, and I don't recognise the confidence in her
demeanour, nor the way her eyes guard her soul. She no longer
needs protection.

I fucking love her.

My rebirth emerges until I can't ignore the tingles in my
toes. They crawl up my legs and swirl in my core. By the time

my awakening has erupted in my psyche, all my fears and shame obliterated, the old Raven has been cleansed, and I'm ready to take on the world.

I know I can do this, because Jamie was right: I am my own defender, my own saviour, and as sure as hell, I will be my own decider.

"Holy fuck." Jamie's standing in the doorway, eyes wide. He swallows hard as his gaze pulls me apart.

I pivot and hold his stare, my voice melting like warm honey. "See something you like?"

He runs both hands through his hair as a deep breath inflates his chest. "Looks like we're all packed."

I glance around the room, strolling through the apartment as I register the soon-to-be memories. The bed where Jamie took my virginity, the tub where dozens of candles burnt as we soaked, the couch where we binged on ice cream and pizzas. Hell, even the Grenadine bottle tucked in the corner of the kitchen waves at me as I grab my cabin luggage.

"I guess I'll be off. I'll catch a bus; it's up the road." I lift the handle and roll the small case towards the door.

Jamie's on my heel. "I'll drop you off. I'm assuming you're staying in the city?"

"Yeah. The Met. But I really don't need you. It's literally five minutes away."

He shakes his head and motions for the front door. "Exactly. It's on my way."

The road map that suddenly appears on his forehead says more than the one-liners he's been throwing my way since we returned. And based on the tight lips, I'd guess he's saving me the lecture on common sense and walking through the Valley at this time of night.

My heart grows heavy as we share the six-minute ride to the club. The lights blind me when we get closer, the music blaring through the streets of the city.

Once pulled over in the parking lot, Jamie turns the ignition off, his gaze focused on the bodies coming in and out of the overpriced, understated hot spot. His fingers strangle the leather of his steering wheel. "You're going to be okay?"

I nod, my lips sewn into a painful mask as I search for the words that never come. My legs are frozen to my seat, and I know I should get out, but I can't. My body stiffens as I wait for him to hug me goodbye.

He doesn't.

Instead, he nods and leans over, until his fingers have disengaged the lock on the passenger side. My car door opens to my new beginning. "Goodbye, Raven."

It's time.

Chapter Eighteen

There's a void in my stomach as I walk away from Jamie's car. I ignore it, forcing my body forward as I march to the front door of the nightclub, pretending I'm not dying to look into his eyes one last time.

New beginning, sister. Just keep walking.

My chest is heavy when I hand over my wrist for the entry stamp to The Met. Vibrations rock me, loud music pulsing through my eardrums. The DJ lights flash in full swing. It takes about thirty seconds for Jess to zone in on me when I step over the threshold, and relief spreads when she pulls me into a hug.

"Finally! Where have you been?" Her bright-red lips shine as she screams over the music. She's wearing a pink strappy dress that's even sexier than mine. She's hot.

"Got delayed coming back." I squeeze her tight. "Long story."

"Tell me all about it," she squeals. She pulls me away from the crowd. "I think it's shit that you couldn't keep your phone though, if you ask me."

A teeny smile crawls on my face when I hear Jamie's ghost in my mind, making the same comment. "Yeah, so I'm told."

She points to a couple of low barstools, and I'm glad for the moment alone with her. I think my wobbly heart needs the girly time. I fall on the seat, my back resting on the brick wall behind me. My muscles are sore and I'm tired, but the thought of spending the night alone in my cold bed makes me want to rip my eyes out with a fork.

"Give it to me, sister. How was it? Did it hurt? Are you glad?"

Jess bombards me with a thousand questions, a glimmer in her pupils, like she's bracing for the most exhilarating news of the year. I suppose, a week ago, this would have been an exciting debrief, even for me. But tonight, I'm not sure. It feels superficial now. There's no way I can translate any of what happened and do it justice.

I inhale a hard breath and let it out slowly, my chin wobbling when the emotions I've been suppressing for the last few hours rocket to the surface.

Jess's eyes grow wide. "Oh my god, sweetie. What's wrong?" Her arms envelop me as she rubs my back.

I lean into her, my shoulders dropping. "I think I got a little too attached."

She swipes the tear rolling down my cheek. "Oh, darl, that's normal. All girls think they have feelings for their first. It goes away though."

"It didn't feel like it was a job." I chuckle a pathetic sound. "I'm being a complete sook."

A grin replaces the concern fading on her face. "You might be, but at least you know. And I'm telling you, once you've done a couple of rounds with your boy, you won't even remember this little escapade."

I know she's right. I'm being a complete drama queen. My

lungs rise a couple of times, and when fresh air has cleared my head, I relax. "Any more drama on campus?"

"Nope. End of term for everyone, and that's all anyone cares about." She purses her lips. "Well, at least for the rest of us. Stella and the guy who took all those photos of her got back together. That drama died pretty quickly after that."

I tilt my head. "You're joking? She went back to him?"

"Yep. Apparently so. I'd have kicked his ass to Norway if you asked me, but whatever. To each their own."

A taste of sympathetic outrage trickles through me, and I freeze when my brain connects the dots.

I think I'd kick his ass too.

I'm glad it didn't happen to me, but right now, I'm pretty sure someone would lose their dick if they thought twice about it.

The new Raven in me dances in front of my face, her eyes narrowed. Pride shines in her glare, the smirk on her face scaring me as I realise she's really a part of me now. "Fucking idiots, the whole lot of them." I laugh as Jess runs a finger across her throat. "Talking about idiots. How's my boyfriend?"

"He's been all right. I think. As all right as Dylan can be. He's excited to see you tonight."

My heart settles, hope teasing, as I picture the possibility of us growing closer. "We better go and find him, right?"

She studies me as I stand, her teeth nibbling at her bottom lip. "Something's different about you, Raven. I just can't put my finger on it."

A smile escapes my heart until it's painted on my pretty little face. "I do feel different." I pull her into my arms. "But thank you for noticing."

When we're all hugged out, she locks her elbow with mine and guides me towards a couple of booths in the main area. The usual crew of students has gathered around a few tables, shots and nibblies spread out amongst them. Though I can only see their backs, I immediately recognise a couple of girls from my graphics class, some guys from the Uni Bar, and in the middle of them, Dylan.

My heart flutters with hope as everyone greets me and I say hello to my guy.

"Hey." He leaps to his feet and gives me a quick peck. He scans my outfit before he downs a tequila shot. "Missed ya around here."

I slide into the booth until I'm seated next to him. "Family business to attend to. Just got back."

"All good. Glad you're here. Missed that ass of yours."

His palm snakes around my waist and lands on the top of my thigh. He winks at the dude in front of him as he squeezes my flesh, almost like they share a type of Morse code I've yet to decipher. I bet it's called Dimwits for Dummies.

Great start, mate.

I ignore the tension building in my shoulders again and shift his hand away from my butt. I lace my fingers through his and redirect his hand between us. Surprise shines in his gaze, but he doesn't challenge me. Instead, he smirks and leans forward until he's whispering in my ear. "Tonight's the night, babe. I'm gonna show you what a real man's made of."

I move back until his whole body's in my line of vision. Tight black pants, crisp lime shirt, gelled hair, Dylan actually scrubbed all right tonight. But as hot as he is, there's something missing.

"Are you now?" I say, humour lacing my tone. "You might want to cut down on those, then." I point to the six empty shots in front of him.

A dark shade of pink colours his cheeks, and Jess gives me a puzzled glance as I high-five my provocative alter. Though, there *is* one thing I'd like to try.

I *just* want to know.

I take a deep breath as my lips land on his neck. He jolts, surprised, but recovers quickly. He turns his head until his mouth meets mine, and within a second, his tongue's sucking like a wet vacuum.

I flinch, almost biting him in the process, and twist my body back towards the group. I grab one of the shots on the table and shove it down my throat, praying to God that it burns whatever's left of Dylan's pressure-hosing.

Nope. Definitely not quite the butterflies.

In Dylan's defence, I'm staring at everyone checking us out, and it feels like I'm putting on a show. I shake the disappointment, bracing for my next move. After all, things might be different if we were relaxed with a bit more privacy.

I *really* have to know.

"Dylan, could I speak to you for a minute?" I ask, my tone as sweet as the left-over cocktails on the table.

His eyes light up. "Of course, buttercup."

He guides me out of the booth, his hand on the small of my back, and leads us to an alcove at the rear of the club. Cold air blows against my skin as we settle on a retaining wall right outside the main building. My ears praise the break from the screeching as my eyes thank the heavens for the dimmed lights, the fresh air, and the privacy.

"Have I told you how horny you make me dressed like that?"

My jaw clenches, and it takes all of my strength not to roll my eyes at the frat-boy comment. "Nope. Not in so many words."

He bends forward and licks the flesh behind my ear. "Well, you do. My dick's hard."

Pinched mouth, I clench my fist to stop my hand from frantically wiping at his spit. It stings and sticks until it feels like I have slugs mating on my neck.

Life in a convent sounds pretty good, right about now.

"All right, all right. Let's try something else." I spread his legs open and slide between them. His eyes twinkle, his mouth open, like he's just won the lottery. I glide my hands over his chest, feeling every groove on his abs, until my arms slither around his neck. "I'm gonna kiss you."

He grins, right before he opens his mouth. Our tongues meet, but in less than three seconds, I'm done. It's like taking a shower on the inside, and a cold one at that.

I just can't.

I sigh and shift until I'm back leaning against the wall. I run a hand across my face, resolution sinking in. I'm as turned on as a dead fish. "I think it might be time for me to go home."

Dylan twists until he's facing me, eyes bulging. His cheeks grow red, his brow furrowed. "You fucking tease," he snarls. "You don't promise a guy some action, then bail at the last minute."

My eyes roll so far up I fear they'll get stuck at the back of my head. "Dylan, we're just not compatible."

He grabs my wrist and pulls it. "Of course, we are. Let me show you."

I yank my arm out of his grip and step back. "I think I'm done here, mate. It's not personal."

"You're just a stupid slut." He's frothing at the mouth. "A fucking frigid bitch, that's what you are."

Beads of sweat pull at the base of my neck, Dylan's words stinging. Maybe he's right. Maybe the clock's struck midnight, and it's time to bury the fairy tale. Hesitation swirls in my mind, thoughts jumbled as I fight the despair clawing back into my soul.

As if he senses it, Dylan softens his hold on me. The red vessels in his eyes settle as he croons, "Babe, why don't you kiss me again, and we'll forget all of this happened?"

But before I have time to process my next move, Dylan's

eyes narrow in the distance. His shoulders square as he spits, "What the fuck are you looking at?"

My heart rate spikes, and I turn to catch a glimpse of a shadow leaning against the side wall. Arms crossed, back propped against the bricks, he tilts his head in silence.

Listening. Watching. Ready to pounce.

Then, as he glides out of the darkness, familiar blue eyes peering, he hisses, "I think it might be time for Dylan to get a little reminder about what consent really is."

Chapter Nineteen

My body feels him in the air before my brain has clicked that Jamie's prowling towards us. His gait is slow, assured.

In control.

I swallow hard, my eyes growing wide, as I stare from one to the other. The two men face each other, Jamie's smooth forehead a contrast to the tight cords around Dylan's collarbone. My heart races in my chest, almost as fast as the vein jackhammering at the base of my *ex*-boyfriend's neck.

"Who the fuck are you?" Dylan growls.

Jamie steps closer until he's only a metre away from us. Hands in his pockets, he puffs a breath as he thrusts his chin forward. "Does it matter?"

"You can just fuck off, dude. It's between me and my girlfriend."

Jamie rolls his eyes. "Clearly." Then, as if Dylan wasn't there, our gazes meet, and he asks, "Are you okay?"

I nod, my throat dry.

He swings his gaze back to Dylan. There's a hardness in

there I've not seen before. "Looks like you've got yourself a dilemma, mate."

Dylan's eyes narrow, his Adam's apple bobbing up and down like it's stuck in some dysfunctional elevator. "And what's that?"

"Learn to respect women, or find yourself wanking alone for the rest of your miserable life."

My mouth opens, but no words come out. My hands grow clammy. Based on the way Dylan clenches his fists, this isn't going to end well.

Panic fills me. "Jamie, no." There're no doubts in my mind that Dylan and I are over, and there will be a price to pay for insulting his ego. Most likely, I'll be crowned the next campus skank, and while I'm not looking forward to it, it's not worth Jamie getting hurt.

He winces when he hears his name, pain flashing over his features as soon as he registers the angst in my tone. "It's okay, Raven." He spins until he's no longer facing me. "Dylan and I... we are just having a friendly man-to-man chat."

Dylan takes a step back when Jamie moves forward. Maybe it's the darkness in his stare, or the way his whole body ripples with each movement, but whatever the reason, Dylan's eyes widen.

"See, you're going at it the wrong way." Jamie's tone lightens. Like a predator toying with his prey, he quietly hovers over Dylan, until Dylan's bouncing on his feet, his adrenaline pumping.

"Fuck off. You have no idea what you're talking about. She's got sex issues, and I'm teaching her to not be such a prude," Dylan stammers, as he goes to grab my hand, but he stops midway when Jamie's glare pins him into place.

"You're teaching *her* about sexual enlightenment?" Jamie's laughter fills the space. It's genuine. Like Dylan said the funniest thing ever. "Jesus, that's priceless. From where I'm standing, it looks like the girl's trying to give you a crash course on Kissing 101."

Dylan's chest rises. "I've never had complaints before."

I fight the cringe twirling in the pit of my stomach, my hands covering my face at the tension building.

"Well, I'll be damned." Sarcasm drips off Jamie's tongue. "You had me fooled."

Dylan squares his shoulders as he pushes himself off the retaining wall. "She's a consenting adult, mate, so you can..."

"Consenting?" Jamie's pitch grows deeper. He shakes his head before he barks, "You're missing the whole point."

Jamie takes a step towards me, his eyes locked on mine. Electricity crackles in the air as he gets closer, and suddenly, it's like we're alone again.

"Consent isn't always in what a woman *says*." His voice drops, the husky sound sending a current to my lower belly. He takes another step until he's standing in front of me. "It's in the way her *body* tells you."

I swallow hard as his finger trails my forearm. I don't register Dylan's jaw dropping next to me. I'm too stunned.

His finger runs higher until it's tracing the curve of my bare shoulder. My nipples harden at his touch. "It's in the way her goosebumps lift her skin." He lowers his face in slow motion until he's murmuring against my neck. "It's in the way her mouth opens for you when she senses your body heat."

Oh god.

There's a stirring in my core I've never experienced before. It sends zaps of sinful pleasure tingling through my being as I'm powerless in Jamie's arms. Next to us, I register Dylan's glare as he observes the pleasure marking my face. The vein at the base of his neck threatens to explode, and it only kicks me into a higher gear. I should tell Jamie to stop. I know I should. And yet, there's no willpower left in me when he runs his hands through my hair and brings his lips to mine.

Warmth reignites in my body as his teeth tug gently on my bottom lip. His tongue dances with mine, taking its time, until I've got my hands fisting his shirt.

I whimper against him as Dylan ceases to exist. "Jamie."

His knee nudges my thighs until he's nestled between them. "The way her legs spread for you. Like you belong between them."

A hard breath whizzes next to us. Dylan's livid, his hands shaking as he's gelled to the spot by the way Jamie approaches then embraces me.

My eyes close, as a need throbs through my centre. It's powerful. Irresistible. It consumes me until time halts around us, and all I have left is Jamie's voice guiding me to my own lighthouse.

He nuzzles his mouth in the soft spot behind my ear. "It's in the way her breath hitches when you first touch her, like she can't wait another second for you to give yourself to her. Like you can read her body as if it were brail, and not miss a single dot. It's owning a key to each other's pleasure without words or instructions."

I fall against his chest, my heart pounding as if it were trying to escape my rib cage. Jamie hoists me up until my legs are locked around his waist. He takes my weight like I'm nothing, his hands cupped under my bottom.

"You know she's with you when she meets you halfway. When her calves are so tight around you that there's no doubt it'll leave a mark the next day."

My fingers beeline to his skull until they're raking through his hair. I pull on it gently as I press a more forceful kiss on his lips, my tongue craving his, like he's lit a fire I can no longer contain. "Don't stop."

Mirroring mine, his eyes are clouded with torment. They're laced with desire, even as hesitation flickers through them.

Jamie's head turns slightly, and I know he's death-staring Dylan. My ex's low growl comes to life when Jamie whispers right above my ear, "It's in the way she whimpers against you and begs you to stay." Then, his voice hardens as he goes for the kill. "Have you got her there, Dylan?"

Jamie's grip on me loosens, and a cold shower takes over when my feet touch the ground again. I miss him already. Slowly, he reaches for my hand, his fingers laced with mine as he pushes me behind him.

My forehead rests on Jamie's back for a second as I catch my breath. He's warm. Solid. Like a cyclone-resistant shelter designed for my heart.

"You..." Dylan stutters as he spits the word. "You have no idea who I am."

"Or I don't fucking care," Jamie says. "But I do care about her. So, let me make myself clear." He releases my hand, and in one stride, he's towering over him. "You just *think* of spreading some fucking bullshit about her in your pathetic study club, and I'll drop you in front of the whole campus, until you're known as the soft-dick bitch for the rest of your pitiful existence. There'll be no coming back from that, got it?"

Dylan pales, jaw tensed, as he nods in Jamie's direction. Then he takes off, disappearing inside the club like he's just seen a ghost.

I crumple on the wall, my legs buckling. Jamie rushes to my side. He pulls my hand into his lap and presses a kiss to my forehead. "I couldn't leave you without saying goodbye properly, and then I heard him..."

A small smile lifts the corner of my mouth. "Thank you."

"I meant everything, Raven. You're an amazing woman. You're strong. You're passionate, and you're definitely the sexiest thing I've ever been with."

An odd sense of peace settles me. "I have to find myself, right?"

He nods and exhales. "You deserve that chance."

The back door of the club smashes against the wall as heels smack the concrete towards us. "Oh my god, Raven. Are you okay?" Jess yells as she lands in front of me.

Jamie lets go of my hand and takes a step back.

She glances towards him, a quizzical look flashing across her face before she pulls me against her chest. "I was so worried. You completely vanished, and I had visions of you dead on a sidewalk."

A chuckle teases me as I squeeze her tight. I'm lucky to have her. "Sorry."

"Saw Dylan take off a little fast. Everything okay?" She narrows her eyes at Jamie, then at me again. "Oh my god. No way. Don't tell me this is the…"

I nod. "Aussie hunk? In the flesh."

Jamie tilts his head in an exaggerated fashion. "Pleasure to meet you."

Jess's lips pucker. "Shit. I see your point," she says to me, her eyes not leaving him. "He's fucking hot."

God Almighty.

She laughs and steps towards the back door again. "All right, since you're safe and everything, I'll give you five. Meet me back inside when you're ready to go?"

When Jamie shifts towards the streetlights, I dash over to him. I grab both of his hands and squeeze them in mine. "Let's say goodbye properly this time, lover boy."

He smiles, the twinkle in his eyes as warm as the sun. "I'd love that." He cups my face with his open palms, his gaze locked on mine, and lowers his face. "Don't ever forget how special you are, beautiful."

Tears well along my lashes, and I fist his shirt as I rein in the building emotions.

I'm ready to say goodbye.

"I won't." My voice breaks. "I'll never forget you."

His lips touch mine. His kiss is soft. Careful. Focused.

As if he's trying to imprint it on his soul. Like the caress of a forbidden lover, Jamie's mouth seals our passion one last time before he wipes a stray tear from my cheek. Then, with a deep breath, he turns away from me and marches into the distance.

I could have sworn there was moisture in his eyes.

Chapter Twenty

M y emails load in the background as I check the final touches on my social media set for Youth Legacy. Banners, graphics, and content—all the perfect blend of colours—are ready for their big open day. What started out as a three-month contract to keep my mind off things feels like a professional epiphany. I think I've found my calling in graphics and social media management, and the extra income doesn't go astray.

I dial April McKenzie's code, and wait for my client to pick up my Zoom call.

Her smile appears on my laptop. "Hi, Raven, I was waiting for our meeting. Can't wait to see what you have for us."

"I think you'll be happy with them," I sing-song. Like I've done this forever, I share my screen until a bunch of logos slide between us and she checks out our final products for her youth centre.

"OMG, I love that one." Her finger twirls in front of her camera. "And that one. Wait, I think I love them all!"

"We can use all the sets for sure," I say, my tone professional. "We'll start scheduling posts on Facebook and Insta first, and see how it goes." I chuckle. "But let's be real. It will go great; there're no doubts. Your open day will be out of this world!"

"You're a life saver. I hope you know how talented you are, Raven. I've given your details to my friends from The Hope Island Private Hospital, and I'd be surprised if they didn't snatch you as well."

Excitement and pride fill me, my confidence boosting with every new referral. It helps that I genuinely love the work, and apparently do well at it.

As soon as the call ends, I sigh with relief, my spine flopping against the back of the couch. My shoulders drop. I flick the TV on, mainly for the white noise, and drag over the laundry basket by my feet. Mechanically, I fold a bunch of t-shirts and pile them on the coffee table in front of me.

My fingers grab the next item, and I cringe at the memories, as my eyes land on the black mini skirt. Date number nine wasn't as traumatic as the one before it, and definitely not the one after, but still... A grin pastes itself on my face as I visualise Eddie's rants throughout the whole dinner ordeal.

I think I'll stick to my vibrator for now.

In the background, the jingle for *The Today Show* chimes, and I give it half my attention as my fingers fold more clothes as fast as they can. I'm off for the whole weekend, and I have a date with a good book I don't want to miss.

The host's voice drones through my apartment, and I catch about every second word until a huge red label with the word 'sex warning' flashes on the screen. I roll my eyes, curiosity poking for my attention.

Don't tell me sex doesn't sell.

"Today's episode promises to be full of controversy as we touch on the subject of sex surrogacy in Australia, and who better qualified than the famous Dr Angela Kendrick to give us her perspective!"

I jerk my head up, my eyes wide and zoning in on Angela strolling through the set of the show. My heart skips a beat.

Oh god.

Wearing a pastel suit, her signature lipstick on, she settles comfortably on a sofa next to the host. Legs crossed, she waves at the audience, relaxed, like she's not completely live on TV.

My blood whooshes in my veins, the sudden pressure aching in my bones. My eyes glance at the purple underwear sitting on top of my washing basket, the memories of my time in her house still fresh in my mind. As I stare at the screen, everything goes blank. My time with Jamie, a little over three months ago, feels like yesterday. I grab the cotton panties, my fingers latching onto the material.

My throat dries as Angela and her host get into chitchats about the state of sexology in the country.

"Angela, why don't you tell us about the difference between sex therapy and sex surrogacy?" the host says, as he takes a quick look at the talking points on the cards in his hands.

"Of course. Well, the first part is pretty easy," she explains. Her tone's as confident as I remember it. "There is no touching in sex therapy, *whatsoever*. In sex surrogacy, there is touching, but it's always for the benefit of the patient."

The host sends an exaggerated wink to the audience. Laughter resonates throughout the stage. "Ooh, and can you tell us where we can get our hands on one of these?"

Angela plays along with the banter. "I could, if it were recognised in Australia. Unfortunately, for us Australians, sex surrogacy is still in the pregnancy stage—which is a complete charade, if you ask me. The work that can be done between a sexologist, a sex surrogate, and a patient is huge."

The crowd sends a dramatic 'boo' through the audience, the host nodding like he's surprised. "Right? We have so many questions about that work and the future of sex surrogacy. Angela, any chance you could introduce us to an expert?"

Angela smiles and opens her hands towards the back of the set. "Absolutely. The best of the best!"

This is so completely staged.

"I'd like to introduce you to my son. James Kendrick."

My stomach lurches in my throat, my breathing growing tight as I watch Jamie pop up on the TV set.

You've gotta be kidding me.

Dark-grey suit, hair slicked back, the same panty-melting smile, he sits across from his mother and their host, completing the perfect triangle. "Thanks for having me."

My heart gallops in my chest, feelings I'd forced down resurfacing as I register the man on my screen. I run a finger along my lips, the phantom of his last kiss lingering.

Like he's ready to feast, the host leans forward and gets straight into it. "James, with a mother like Angela, I'm guessing this was a natural career progression for you. How did sex surrogacy happen?"

Jamie clears his throat, and he and Angela exchange a quick glance before he answers. "I trained in America. In the state I was in, the work was legal and regulated. It was pretty clear-cut."

The host shuffles more cards in his hands. "Angela, you were telling us that sex surrogacy doesn't exist *per se* in Australia. How does this work here, then?"

Angela's lips pucker. "Exactly. Sex surrogacy in Australia can't happen the way it's intended. So, workers have to be creative. They can call themselves sexual bodyworkers, or sex workers, and still follow the framework of sex surrogacy, but only people in the field would really know the difference."

"Good point. James, what difference does it make for commoners like us?" the host asks, an eyebrow cocked.

My fingers wring the cotton underwear between my

hands. The material twists with every gasp ripping from my lungs.

Jamie takes a deep breath, and his tone comes to life. There's passion in his words. "It's huge. For starters, there're no regulating bodies, no recognised codes of ethics, no boundaries. The only code is a moral one, so that leaves the clients at the mercy of the professionals working with them."

"No rules at all?" The host opens his mouth to the camera. His whole face fills the screen.

"No. Not legally."

Angela lifts a finger in the air and gets the host's attention. "Hence, why it's even more important to rely on a strong moral compass." Her eyes turn to her son, care glowing in her gaze. "I'm proud to say that Jamie has stuck to his own boundaries, and always puts the women he works with first and foremost, regardless of how backwards we are in the sex therapy field in Australia."

The crowd 'awwwws' loudly, Jamie's face growing blank, like this wasn't in the script.

"Really?" the host says. "Give us your golden rules, James."

Jamie's chest rises, his fingers curling in and out of his palms, as he processes his response. Then, the line between his brows softens. "We know, from research, that it takes about eight to twelve weeks for the clients to move out of the lust cloud and back into real life. Until then, they can have all of these feelings they think are real, and it gets messy. And the last thing I'd want to do is take advantage of that."

"So, what you're saying is: you're nipping any power differential in the bud, by severing all future contact with these women after you part ways."

"Yes." Jamie's voice is low. Based on the way he wipes his palm on his pants, there's anxiety coursing through him over where this is going.

"Wow. Has anyone come forward after that time?"

My eyes grow heavy with unshed tears as the puzzle pieces fall into place. It all makes sense now. His work ethics. The torment his eyes held as he left me at The Met. The dozens of comments about me finding myself.

It was all about protecting me.

"Of course not. It's not in the order of things." There's a sadness lacing his tone, and the light in his eyes has dulled.

My body's frozen on the couch, my brain pulling Jamie apart in my head. His smiles, his hugs, his caring words. Even the way he dropped me off a freaking cliff. My heart bleeds from not being able to touch him right now. And it's not remotely sexual.

My chest shatters into a thousand pieces, and I pull my arm across my middle, hoping to soothe the void growing in my stomach. I'm in love with this man, and all I want is to hold him, like he held me, until the light's back in his gaze.

My pulse pounces faster as I skim through my emails.

There it is!

Natalie's monthly reminder of my outstanding voucher opens, the black and gold cursive logo flashing in front of my eyes. Fingers shaking, I dial her number. She answers almost immediately.

"Hi, Natalie, this is Raven." I take a breath, hoping to steady the pitch in my voice.

"OMG, I had given up on you," she croons on the other end of the line. "It's so good to hear from you."

I clear my throat, butterflies growing in my stomach. "Listen, I was wondering..."

"No need to ask," she interrupts me. "I've got you, sister. Daniel is all yours whenever you're free." She rustles some papers in the background as she hums. "How does Friday sound?"

The butterflies in my belly grow, until they feel more like

cramps than anything else. "No, no. Sorry," I say. My blood rushes through my ears, until even I can't hear the sound of my own voice. "I was hoping to catch up with Jamie."

The rustling stops. "Oh."

Silence stretches between us.

Then she sighs. "I'm afraid that's not possible, darl. Jamie resigned almost four months ago."

Chapter Twenty-One

The drive to Kingscliff drags on longer than I remember. I guess that's what happens when there's no entertainment on the road.

The closer I get to the Kendricks' estate, the more my brain screams that I'm a complete moron and to turn the hell back.

If he wanted to see you, he would have told you.

I take a deep breath, my kick-ass alter praising me for my latest bold behaviours. I've gone on dates, opened my own mini business, and completely blocked Dylan and his crew from my life. So, what's a little surprise trip through the New South Wales's border in comparison?

I swallow hard, my fingers clenching the steering wheel as I approach the cul-de-sac of the Kendricks' property. The estate looms, the black gates as daunting as ever.

My tyres crunch as I drive over the sidewalk and park the car in a quiet spot. Eyes closed, I focus on deep breathing, exhaling the air from my belly until the shaking in my limbs is somewhat manageable.

Stop being a coward.

The car door closes behind me, and I flinch at the loud click. Everything in this scenario screams *break in*. The white jeans, the sunglasses, even the soft runners. It's like I'm bracing for a quick exit; all I'm missing is the combination of the safe and where to find the twenty-four carat diamonds.

I expect the cops to barge in any minute, but nothing happens when I turn the knob of the side gate and make my way to the front porch.

Ten... Nine... Eight...

I count backwards with every step, my mind zeroed in on the scenery around me. It doesn't feel that long ago that I was here, yet March's cooler skies have replaced December's warm air. I tighten the wrap around me. Everything's greener now.

Seven... Six... Five...

The smell of fresh grass lingers, my senses keeping me grounded to the moment. Anything to avoid a freak out at the last minute. My strides grow more confident as I relax into the memories of this place.

Three... Two... One...

It takes about three minutes for me to get up the driveway, and I'm only semi-surprised when Angela meets me at the door, her finger pointing to the camera above her head. Arms casually crossed, a massive grin on her face, she leans against the white column as she greets me. "I wondered whether we'd ever see you again." She rushes down the stairs to meet me halfway.

"I'm sorry. I would have called..." I tug on my earlobe. "But I had no contact details, and..."

I'm interrupted by Angela's arms squeezing me tight. She holds me for a second longer than she has to.

"I'm so glad you did." She motions me up the stairs. "He doesn't know, does he?"

A nail goes to my mouth, and I inhale, praying to God now's not the time when Angela calls for security to escort me out. "I saw the show yesterday."

She smiles, a motherly grin that reaches her eyes. "He's in the woods." Then, she rubs my shoulder and points to the clearing at the back of the house. "Raven, go and get your answers, sweetheart."

In a flash, I'm alone again, staring at the mental path laid out in front of me. My memories of Jamie are special moments I'll cherish forever. While a part of me wants nothing more than to hold him again, the other part is petrified.

He could still reject you.

I shake the thoughts buzzing in my mind, and start the trek to find out for myself. Because until I do, he's ruined me for everyone else.

Since he left me that night, Jamie's everywhere. His phantom smell lingers on my pillow and it's his voice I hear when I'm feeling vulnerable. His face is etched in my mind, like a guardian angel, his blue eyes piercing through my soul. And though I haven't seen him in almost four months, it feels like he's never very far.

Excitement sends pins and needles to my extremities, and I fist my hands, apprehension building the closer I get.

You've got this.

My mind clears when I get to the top of the meadow. It's as pretty as I remember. Thousands of wildflowers welcome me as I step through the grassland, the same sweet smell floating around. It sends a shot of serenity to my overactive brain. My steps feel lighter, and filled with hope, I look up, my face absorbing the sunrays shimmering in the clearing.

Warmth charges me until I'm one with the sun, my strength intensifying until I know my heart like never before.

I'd rather be rejected than spend the rest of my life wondering about the what ifs.

When my gaze lowers, Jamie's shadow is in the distance. Apprehension is replaced by excitement. And I float forward, my steps more determined with each stride until I'm just a couple of metres behind him.

My heart drums rhythmically, the loud thumps reminding me that there's no going back.

He's really here.

Jamie's perched on a large boulder. So close, and yet so far. His back to me, he's drafting something on a sketch pad with what looks like charcoal, his fingers gliding over the paper like he's speaking in tongues. He's fast. Sharp. Focused. His forearm twitches below the white shirt folded to his elbows, and with every stroke, passion bleeds through his stare.

My breathing hitches at the beauty of the man. I feel unworthy of the intrusion. It's like I've snuck myself into the intimate moment, and I'm suspended in this space, unable to cross the distance between us.

The air crackles, and I swallow hard, my body betraying me. Words won't form. They're stuck in my throat as my eyes decipher the drawing coming to life.

I gasp.

It couldn't be...

Jamie's head jerks back when the leaves crunching underfoot resonate in the meadow. Our eyes meet, and in complete silence, he studies me like I'm a piece of art. He remains motionless, less than a metre away from me, eyes bright, his arms fused against his thighs.

His fingers stir, the sketch pad on his lap plunging between his legs. The picture sways in the wind until it lands by my feet. I lower my gaze to the black and white portrait. And my own eyes, smeared in charcoal, stare back at me. My throat tightens as I lift the paper from the ground and take the step that separates us.

My feet feel like lead, every stride scarier than the last. My fingers clench the page until I'm so close to Jamie I can almost touch him. My heart burns in my chest.

He slides himself forward until his legs meet the ground. He moves slowly, like he's afraid I'll disappear. Then, without a word, he lifts his hands and cups my face, his forehead resting on mine.

I curl against his chest until I'm nestled in his arms. Emotions build, and I fight them as he closes his eyes and brings his lips to mine.

His kiss is slow. Loving. *Vulnerable.* As if he's floating after being chained down for so long.

Relief flickers on his face when I lay my cheek against his chest. His heartbeat throbs through my flesh.

"I missed you," I murmur.

"I missed you too," he says back, his voice thin.

A million questions float in my mind, but only one burns my tongue like a hot iron. How does he feel about me now that the job's over? What does his heart say as I'm in his arms again?

Does he feel the way I feel?

Sheltered by his warmth, it's almost easy to daydream what it is I want to hear. And yet, the trembling in my core knows that I just need the truth.

Whatever it might be.

"I don't want you to feel guilty or worry about me. I'm okay," I whisper in his ear. "I just had to know whether I saw something that didn't exist."

His tone breaks as he holds me tighter. "Baby, you're all I think about. Leaving you there that night, not knowing whether you were happy or even safe killed me. I'm sorry I messed up. I completely crossed all the professional lines ever drawn." He takes a deep breath, and exhales. When he's regained his composure, he continues, "I had to let you experience things for yourself. You deserved a chance at a new beginning, without you thinking you could only exist to give guys whatever they wanted."

Tears slide down my cheeks, my heart bursting with the emotions I have for him. I know it makes no sense. I barely know him. And yet, my heart beats with his. In perfect sync.

I love him.

"I understand now. Everything you said was true." I lean back until I'm staring into his eyes. "I want you more, now that I know I don't *need* you or anyone else. I'm worthwhile, even on my own."

His pupils lighten. "You're more than worthwhile, Raven. You're perfect as you are. You're beautiful and you're caring, and I'm fucking head over heels for you." Invisible music plays as we slow dance in each other's arms. "I love the powerful woman you've become." A soft kiss lands on my nose. "But I love the fragile side of you, the slice I get to keep for myself. The part I can hold and protect like I'm some goddamn caveman." Another peck grazes me. "I love everything about you. Because with you, it's different. It's loving life. It's having faith that we're going to love every minute of it as equals. Being with you is as easy as existing in the same air. And nothing beats that, Raven. Nothing at all."

I blink with unshed tears, my heart singing at the most beautiful words anyone's ever said to me. "Jamie," I murmur against him as I tighten my arms around his waist.

"I love you, beautiful girl."

"I love you too, Jamie Kendrick." Salty drops roll down my cheeks, and I lean forward to kiss him. "When did you know?"

He sighs, his chin resting on the top of my head. His hands rub my shoulders as he holds me close. "When I told Mum's driver not to bring the car back until four. There was no reason to delay our trip back, other than me being a selfish bastard and wanting you for another full day."

I push away, the smirk on my face growing as depth colours his cheeks. "Oh my god, you did it on purpose?"

He laughs. "Yep. All so I could see your face when I dropped you from that cliff. Fuck, that was hot."

"You know, for the rest of my life I'll pretend it wasn't, right?" I chuckle.

"And we'll both know you're lying." His breath tickles my ear. "It'll be our little secret."

We cuddle in silence for a minute, the intensity of the moment sinking in. Then, I bring my hand up, my portrait now between us. "This is so beautiful."

"Art therapy, compliments of Dr Angela Kendrick." His fingers trace the charcoal silhouette. "Apparently, it was to help process everything that went wrong."

"Or that went right," I say, a tender smile curling my lips. "Does she know?"

"Didn't take her long to work it out. She whipped me for five minutes, and then helped me realise my career as an escort was over."

"You guys have the weirdest relationship." I chuckle, my head shaking at the visual. "But I'm glad I don't have to picture you as Brisbane's favourite Aussie hunk anymore."

His lips brush mine. "A career as a sex educator is something we've talked about, and I'm excited to look into it. But, baby, make no mistake. From now on, I'm only one person's Aussie hunk, and that's yours."

My mouth opens, his tongue dancing with mine. It's warm. Tingly. Like I'm safe again. It takes a second before my body opens to him, my mind and soul blending with his. And when I whimper against him, my doubts and fears vanish. All that's left is freedom.

Freedom to love him, worship him, and stand by him as the kick-ass woman I always was. *I just didn't know it.* But with Jamie by my side, I'm ready to take on the world, and he sure as hell will make certain I never forget it.

Epilogue

EIGHT WEEKS LATER

J amie looks dashing in his dark-navy dress pants and white button-up shirt. The top button's undone, his forearms bare to his elbows. Next to him, Dr Jarryd Williams, my friend April's man, whispers something in his ear as they brace themselves to teach a sex-ed session to the kids from Youth Legacy.

"Are you sure these kids are ready for this?" I ask April, my eyes never leaving Jamie.

She nods. "Yep. There's no time like the present, to learn life skills. Thanks so much for organising this, Raven. We're pumped."

I turn towards her and smile. "Our pleasure. He's passionate about the topic, so it's definitely not a chore to him."

When the group grows quiet, Jamie clicks on his first slide and waits in complete silence as the teenagers in front of him gasp. A collage of naked bodies flashes across the screen. All different ages, unique shapes, and abilities. Then he clicks on the next slide, and images of various couples appear, in assorted stages of beautiful intimacy.

My eyes study the photo of a man wiping a tear rolling down his partner's face. There's a simple beauty to this image that melts my heart, and that's because I know what that feels like too. Goosebumps crawl along my skin as I'm overwhelmed with love. I take a deep breath and wait for Jamie to continue.

"I'm pretty sure if I asked any of you what sex is, you'd be able to tell me how it works, right?" he asks the kids, his body relaxed as he stands in front of the giant screen. "Who wants to give it a shot?"

Giggles follow, and a girl tosses an answer into the group. "Penis in vagina!"

Jamie nods. "Yep. That's what the world would have you believe. Let's dig a little deeper. What other things could sex be?"

A different kid pipes up, "Oral. Anal. Fingers."

"Yep. All of these things are sexual." He throws some chocolate bars in the air, and the kids launch themselves at the treats as they laugh. "But you're a smart bunch. Let's dig even deeper."

A couple of new slides come on, and this time Jamie has individual photographs. Men and women doing their own thing. He pauses the screen on a guy standing in his boxers in a bathroom. "What about single people? What's sex to them?"

"Tinder!" a voice yells at the back.

The group explodes into laughter.

Jamie smirks. "Are you telling me that sex is only with two people? You guys think it's fair that a single person can't enjoy pleasure, unless they have a partner?"

Next to me, April murmurs, "Wow. He's good. He's got their attention."

Pride fills me as I watch him in action. He's in his element.

"Yeah. There's nothing they'll throw at him he's not heard before."

"What about consent? Who's game enough to give this a go?" Jamie leans against a large desk, as he folds his arms and waits.

When no one volunteers, a boy with beautiful olive skin stands up. He looks older than his years. "Without consent, there shouldn't be sex—*full stop*."

"Riley?" Jamie squints at the kid's name scrawled on his name tag. "You've just won today's contest."

A whole bag of bite-size treats lands in the kid's arms. He grins and shares a couple of the bars with the kids around him.

"Consent is about checking that your partner's as much into it as you are. It's as easy as asking them whether they like something or prefer something else. Sometimes, young people might be weirded out by speaking up, so it's important to check consent through body language too."

Riley smirks. "So, if I kiss a girl and she runs off to brush her teeth, I'm guessing that's a *no*?"

The teenagers crack up laughing, and Jamie's eyes crinkle as he nods. "Pretty much."

"What's the difference between love and lust?" April's boyfriend asks from Jamie's side.

Jamie's lip twitches, but he doesn't turn. It's almost as if he expected it. He paces amongst the kids as he holds his answer until he's in front of me. "That's a great question, Dr Williams."

Something's off in the way Jamie stares at me. I swallow hard, the question running through my gaze. He ignores me.

What's he up to?

"At the beginning, lust and love can feel a little bit the same. They're both warm and fuzzy. They make us feel butter-flies. Make us hard in all the right places." Jamie glances towards the kids as he grabs my hand. "For a little while, this woman here made me feel like I was a teenager again. I mean, look at her. She's beautiful."

Heat creeps up my neck when the kids croon and 'aww' in the background.

His fingers lace with mine. "But once we went our separate ways, she's all I thought about. I couldn't get her out of my head. It was like a dark cloud took hold of my days. They all looked bleak, and nothing mattered anymore. Nothing felt the same."

My heart rate spikes as a bunch of girls behind him raise their hands to their faces, their mouths forming *O*s. I turn towards April, my eyes pleading for a clue, but instead of filling me in, she takes a step back until she's nestled against Jarryd. And I'm left staring at Jamie's pale face as he kneels in front of me.

Oh my god...

My throat tightens, shock freezing me on the spot. White dots fill my vision, my brain refusing to process the scene unravelling at my feet.

"Love is refusing to live one more day without her. It's having only one purpose in life, and that's to build a future where she has everything she needs and everything she wants. Love is being at peace, knowing you're okay with dying to protect her. Because your mind would combust at the thought of her being in pain. Love is being vulnerable." He gulps. "And putting all of your fears, shame, and insecurities out there. Because you know in your heart that she'll be there with you, through the good and the bad, in sickness and in health, as much as you'll be there for her for the rest of her life."

Tears fill my eyes, and when Jamie pulls a velvet box out of his pocket, they fall freely as I gasp. My fingers cover my mouth as I stare, wide-eyed.

"Raven, I love you so much it hurts. There's not one day that goes by where I don't thank God for having you by my side." He opens the small box and presents me with the most beautiful solitaire I've ever seen. "The only life I want now is a life with you. Would you do me the honour of becoming my wife, for now and forever?"

My heart explodes into a thousand pieces as a sob shakes me. The noise in the room quietens until only a few whispers echo, and all I can hear is my heartbeat screaming *yes*.

I shuffle in my chair until his breath tickles my neck. Our foreheads touch as my hands cup his cheeks. "I love you so much."

Jamie's voice breaks as he whispers, "Baby, will you marry me?"

I wipe the tears cascading down my face with the back of my hand, my lips wobbling as I answer, "Yes, lover boy. I want to be yours forever."

I launch myself into his arms, and he grips onto me as he gives me a final kiss. Then, as we get back on our feet, he pulls the diamond out of the small holder. By the time he slides the ring onto my finger, we're surrounded by the kids, April, and Jarryd—clapping and hugs galore.

It's stunning. It scintillates with every stroke of my hand, and more than anything, I love how it represents the incredible feelings we have for each other.

I knocked on his door, wanting a quick fix for something that didn't matter in the end. Although I didn't know it, losing my virginity never made me a woman. What did was being loved for all the deeper parts of me, until I was healed and strengthened as a unique soul. With my own likes and dislikes. And my own dreams and desires. Jamie's true gift was allowing me to find myself beneath the weight of my darkness, knowing there was a strong woman buried inside. Ready to fight the world as she emerged a powerful force. With or without a man by her side.

His second gift was waiting for me to come home to him when I'd found *her*.

And as we begin our life together, I definitely have.

Do you need more of Jamie and Raven? Get your bonus Epilogue here - **Beautiful Enigma, Wedding.**

The End

Forbidden Promise

Check out the next page for a SNEAK PEEK of Forbidden Promise

Book 1 in The Hope Island Series

Available now on **Amazon**

Why does forbidden fruit always taste the sweetest?

JARRYD

As a doctor, I take my promise "to do no harm" very seriously, which is how I find myself pressured into court-ordered therapy. I might have to sit on her couch and listen to her probing questions, all while imagining her long legs wrapped around my waist or draped over my shoulders, but that doesn't mean I have to bare my soul.

APRIL

I've been slaving away at the local clinic, biding my time until I can register as a private therapist. Nothing is going to take my eyes off the prize. Not even the sexy new patient lounging on the couch in my office. Sure, he's hot, and I'd like to take him for a spin. But the price of crossing that professional line is too high, and the cost is my dream.

When the truth reveals itself, will they keep their forbidden promise? Or will it shatter, along with their hearts?

Chapter One

JARRYD

Bracing my elbows on the mahogany table of the Brisbane Magistrate Court, I cradled my forehead. How had things gone so awry?

Next to me, Eddie, the lawyer my boss recommended, rummaged through paperwork. "It's not too late to change your mind." His clipped tone reinforced his disapproval.

"Say it one more time, and I swear to God I'll hire another solicitor." I sighed, then softened my voice. "I can't put the kid in danger, Eddie. I can't."

The middle-aged man closed the manila folder in front of him. "God, you're not making it easy for me. It's your career in jeopardy, you know?"

I exhaled, the weight on my chest growing heavier. Eddie had a point, but the alternative was to name-drop the kid who'd been in my car that week. And name-dropping the fourteen-year-old son of a gang leader was out of the question. He had limited hope for the future as it was, without adding his deadbeat father hunting him down to the mix.

At least I could afford legal representation. I'd kick Riley's ass soon enough. Outside court. Away from that yellow brick road leading him to jail, like his father, and grandfather before him.

"All rise," the bailiff called. The crowd hushed as the magistrate crossed the room and settled on the black leather, high-backed chair.

I glanced behind at Mom. She smoothed her skirt and clasped her hands. Her usual blonde ponytail had been replaced with a high bun, her grey suit emphasizing the blue of her eyes. She gave me a tender smile before motioning for me to turn.

My career as a doctor was in the balance, but unlike Eddie, Mom understood. Dad would have done the exact same thing.

"Please be seated," the bailiff called again.

Judge Ethan crossed his arms before addressing me directly.

"Dr Williams, we've heard your plea, and while I accept that you claim the hundred and fifty grams of marijuana found in your car wasn't yours, given the fact that you've refused to provide the officer with any more details, I have no choice but to question your circumstances. Care to explain further?"

"I understand, Your Honour. If I knew how these drugs made their way to my car, I would let you know. But I don't. I can only hope that the character references I have provided the court will attest to my integrity, both as a citizen and as a doctor."

Judge Ethan nodded towards my lawyer. Eddie took a breath, buttoned the jacket of his Armani suit, and stood behind the desk. His fingers clung to the pencil he was holding, his knuckles growing white. Clearly, he wasn't used to arguing a defence he disagreed with.

"Your Honour, Dr Williams is at the onset of his career—a

career he has worked hard for. His parents both dedicated their lives to helping others as health professionals, and as evidenced by the character references provided to you, the Williams family is well known by their patients for taking a hard line against drug abuse. Unfortunately, Dr Matthew Williams passed away three years ago—"

Mom and I exchanged a glance, her face paling. She looked as tense as I felt.

"Since then, Jarryd has dedicated countless hours of volunteering with disadvantaged youths in care. He has done as much as he could to prevent the spread of violence as well as the use of illegal and illicit substances. My client is not a drug dealer." Eddie paced behind the desk like he was presenting a case to the Supreme Court.

Our eyes met. Mine, narrowed to slits. His, twinkling over his smug face.

Judge Ethan palmed the gavel on the counter to challenge Eddie. "Dr Williams may not be a drug dealer, but if he's a user, don't we have a responsibility in providing him with rehab, Mr Harper?"

Mom cleared her throat at the judge's question. I didn't have to turn around to know she was willing me to keep it together. Only she knew how much that implication would irk me.

Watching as families were torn apart, kids dying in dark alleys, and the cycle of poverty that followed drug addiction drove me crazy and broke my heart. I hated addicts, dealers, and illegal substances altogether. The mere fact that anyone asked this of me made me want to scream.

No, I wasn't a drug dealer, nor an addict. I was a mentor for a bunch of teens, who'd left their stash behind in my car. For fuck's sake, they needed role-modelling, not criminal records.

My jaw locked, my fists clenched, and when my back straightened, Eddie got the hint. His face and tone lightened.

"No, Your Honour. Dr Williams is not a drug user, nor has he ever been. The urine screen provided to you will attest to this." Eddie handed the test results to the bailiff.

The sample had been taken in a pathology clinic last week. No joke, the whole setup was Jail Prep 101. First the locked basin, then the toilet paper glued around the seat, and finally the middle-aged woman staring at my dick for the three minutes it took me to fill the container. God, Eddie's plan had better work.

"Right." Judge Ethan fiddled with the piece of paper. "I'm still unconvinced that these drugs planted themselves in your car, Dr Williams." He brought his hands together in front of his chest. His hard focus scrutinised the back of the room slowly, before his gaze landed on me again.

My fingers clung to the table.

For a minute, he reminded me of Principal Willoughby, the last time I was in his office, right before we left the States fifteen years ago. Asking me questions to which he already knew the answers. Testing me. Giving me a way out. In this case, the way out was to throw a kid under the bus. A kid the system had already given up on. A kid the media would notice less than a doctor, if charged with drug possession. Particularly given his family history.

I wondered whether the boy had come forward. My head jerked back as I skimmed over the crowd.

At the rear of the courtroom, Riley sat quietly, his hands between his knees. His eyes were red and swollen. Instead of his usual spikes, he'd parted his black hair to the side. He wore his big brother's white shirt, the one they shared for interviews and special occasions. The same faded-blue mark stained his front pocket. His eyes met mine for a brief second, enough to see them glistening.

Just as I turned back, Mom snuck herself near the boy. She gave him that look, that *we-will-talk-about-this-later* glare she used to give me growing up. She nodded, urging me to focus back on the case.

"My client understands, Your Honour. We ask that you consider his lack of prior convictions, his status in his community, and the work he has undertaken both as a doctor and as a youth mentor. We would like to request that Your Honour grants my client the benefit of the doubt, considering that all evidence points to the fact that the drugs were not his."

Judge Ethan grabbed the paperwork in front of him and levelled the pages into an even pile. Slowly. As if my fate was written down on the sheets of paper. When he looked up, he'd made his decision.

"Dr Williams, considering the facts outlined by Mr Harper, your genuine reputation, and the drastic impact that such a conviction would have on your career, I am mandating you to attend six drug-diversion sessions within the next six months. There will be no criminal charges documented on your record as long as you complete the program."

Murmurs buzzed in the room.

"This will address any doubts that I still have regarding whose drugs these were. This will also reinforce the seriousness of these charges. Dr Williams, should more drugs be found in your possession, you will be prosecuted to the full extent of the law. Am I making myself clear?"

"Absolutely, Your Honour. Thank you." I nodded and turned to my smart-ass lawyer.

His lips curled all the way to his ears. God, I didn't always agree with that man, but no one could deny his ability to win even the most unlikely of cases.

I extended my hand. He shook it. "Let's get out of here." Eddie led me to the rear of the courtroom, acknowledging a few people along the way.

I followed him through the large doors leading to the front of the building. Mom leaned on a white pillar, her forehead smoother than it had been thirty minutes ago. Riley fidgeted by her side, his eyes cast to the ground.

My mother rushed towards me, and I pulled her into an embrace.

"Don't ever scare me like that again," she whispered, planting a kiss on my cheek.

"Thanks for looking after Riley." I thrusted my chin towards the teen standing twenty metres away from us. His olive complexion had taken on a pale tone, and he hugged himself like he was expecting a beating. "He's just as freaked out as we are."

"He should be," Mom said. "Go and talk to him."

We moved closer to the lawyer and the teen waiting for us on the footpath. Hopefully, this was the last time these two would meet.

"Riley, take a walk with me?" I motioned towards the park behind the courthouse.

"Yes, sir." Riley followed me, making sure to leave some distance between us. Years of abuse did that to this kid. It's like he was preparing for the worst. Despite his brave façade, his lip wobbled underneath his wispy moustache. The further we strode, the smaller his body looked. By the time we reached a private area, Riley had surrendered to whatever punishment was coming his way.

"Riley, I won't lie." I touched his shoulder softly. "Those drugs could have got me in deep trouble. They were yours, right?"

The boy's voice filled with emotion. "Yes, sir."

"Do you know why I didn't turn you in?" I lowered myself to his eye level, my tone as calming as I could make it.

The fourteen-year-old, the kid who'd come to court with the nicest shirt he owned, shook his head. Stripped from his usual attitude and his mobster lifestyle, the boy in front of me was just a child.

"Because I believe in you, Riley. There is no part of me that doubts you can be whatever you want to be in life."

Tears filled his eyes. He wiped them as soon as they escaped.

"I want to be here for you. But you have to let me. And you have to give me your word that there will never be drugs involved—*ever again*."

"I swear, Jarryd." He threw himself at me and we hugged for a second, then he pushed away.

I chuckled. "All right. You better get home." Half the day had gone by. "I'll see you on Wednesday afternoon. Remember your word."

Riley jogged to the bus stop without turning back.

Mom stepped beside me. "Will he be okay?"

It wasn't clear how long she'd been watching us. Eddie was nowhere in sight. "Yeah. I just wish I could move him out of that environment, you know?"

"One day. For now, let's talk about these diversion sessions."

"I don't even really know what they are, but given Eddie's victory sneer, they can't be that bad."

We made our way back to the carpark.

"No, they're not that bad. But it's serious. You have to follow through." Mom arched an eyebrow.

"Why the hell are you looking at me like that? I can manage a couple of educational sessions on drugs, Mother."

"Son, according to Eddie, you've been mandated to attend therapy, not educational sessions."

My head snapped back. "You can't be serious?"

I paused mid-step. A couple eyed us as they strolled passed, a few seconds going by before my feet shuffled forward again.

I'd spent the last three years of college refusing counselling after Chuck died—*as if talking things out would weaken my soul.*

"No way."

She sighed and grabbed my forearm. When she turned to face me, our common pain was etched in the fine lines around her eyes.

There was a reason I'd chosen not to talk about it. It scared me. Remembering my pain, and how I'd failed the people I loved, petrified me beyond comprehension.

Visions of Chuck's body lying on the cold floor hit me every night. And to make them go away, every morning, a new kid made the list in my youth mentoring team. Some called it avoidant behaviour, I preferred to look at it as *a proactive attitude*.

"You can, Jarryd, and you will. Six sessions, and this nightmare is over." Her tone left no room for argument, and she squeezed my hand twice, willing me to give it a go.

Within seconds, the crushing weight on my chest stole my breath, and every muscle in my body tensed. The need to release my frustration became unbearable. But instead, I just squeezed my mother's hand back.

Fuck me dead. Riley, you owe me.

Chapter Two

APRIL

The clock ticked louder with every second that passed. I finished typing the cover letter. At this rate, the tips of my fingers would be numb before the application for the clinic's social work mentoring program was ready to go.

Third time lucky. This year I'm getting in.

"I don't see the appeal." Grace pivoted her chair towards me. "You're getting yourself frantic over a program that gives you more work, and no pay raise. Seriously, why the desperation?" The dietitian stared at me with a lopsided grin.

I sighed, returned to my screen, and resumed typing. "Imagine you had the chance to be part of a health initiative, guaranteeing you a registration under Medicare. You still reckon you wouldn't want it?"

"Yeah, I guess, but it's a huge commitment. If I was going to volunteer my time for twelve months, on top of my existing full-time job, I'd make it worthwhile. Not spend it dealing with social cases." She tucked her blonde bangs behind her ears. "Or does this sudden interest have anything to do with the new director of social work?" She wagged her eyebrows before returning to her own desktop.

"I'm just going to ignore you now," I teased.

Though he was charming, cute and clearly smart, Simon had nothing to do with my desire to help people. I'd never got the support I needed after Mum and Dad's accident, which could've helped Pops and Grams deal with a twelve-year-old girl who refused to speak for a year. They'd done a wonderful job, but it didn't take away the fact that I grew up very lost. I didn't want others to experience the same hardships.

My fingers rubbed the long scar running down my forearm, the phantom pain still burning.

I should have died with my parents in that car, but I hadn't. So, in the spirit of *what doesn't kill you makes you stronger* and all that... the least I could do was become a source of support for others.

Every January, for the last three years, I'd applied for this bloody program. And every year, my application had been rejected by the previous director. But this year, Simon had personally encouraged me to give it another go.

I'd be damned if I failed this time, even if it meant being a little more *social* than usual. My eyes glanced over the red mark on the calendar pinned to the wall. *Friday night drinks with the social work department.* The appointment taunted me from a distance. In my three years at this clinic, this was the first time I'd been brave enough to network. An antisocial social worker? It had to be seen to be believed, and yet, here I was. I blamed being raised by grandparents in the middle of rural New South Wales.

"Hi, ladies, what are we up to?" Luke, the occupational therapist on our team, sing-songed as he strolled in. He tossed his sports towel on his desk.

"Hey, Luke. How was the exercise group?" Grace's eyes remained on her screen.

"Good. Sally finally decided to join us. A positive sign if you ask me. First time she got out of bed in a week, so I deserve the mental health clinician award of the year, if I say so myself."

"Seriously? You reckon the meds she's on haven't helped at all? Oh, wait, maybe it was my amazing counselling session yesterday," I said, mocking both Grace and Luke.

Luke scoffed. "Yeah, right." He leaned over and took a sneak peek of the document open on the screen. "If it's so good already, why are you applying to join the hippy club?"

Grace chuckled and lifted her palm in the air. Luke slapped it.

"Yeah, April." Grace's fingers tapped her desk. "Why *are* you joining the hippy club?" Her eyes narrowed as she teased me again.

I crossed my arms, squaring my shoulders as much as my small athletic frame could. "That's it. You two are banned from talking to me for the rest of the afternoon. And when my very successful private practice opens, I'll make sure you don't get hired as part of the allied health team."

They both ignored me as they exchanged grimaces, and I pretended it wasn't funny.

The truth was, I agreed with them for the most part—*and they knew it.* Half of the social work department was filled with middle-age women in flowery dresses, who'd spent their careers filling out forms and liaising with child protection. The other half contained hippies with a huge chip on their shoulder. I didn't fit in with either crowd.

There was more to social work, especially mental health social work. Therapies of all kinds were what interested me. Not paperwork, forms, and other practical problems. I wanted to make a *real* difference.

My plan was all laid out. After working in the therapy clinic for a year, there would be enough experience and practice points on my application for accreditation as a mental health social worker. Medicare would recognise me, a private practice would feature my name, and the self-help books I planned on writing would earn multiple awards.

All would be well. According to my perfectly thought-out strategy.

"Right. No more distractions," I mumbled as the other two packed their bags for the day. By the time the clock struck five, the allied health department was eerily quiet, despite the patients and nursing staff on the other side of the wall.

Another hour later, my eyes scanned the printed application. Clear titles, comprehensive rationale, three years' experience working in mental health, and a commitment to twelve months of overtime for free. It was all there, ready to be hand-delivered to my new director of social work.

The clicks of my heels resonated in the empty corridor. Between the silence and the darkness on this side of the building, my heart galloped like a racehorse by the time I got to Simon's threshold.

The light in his office was on, the door ajar. I rapped my knuckles on the wood panelling a couple of times. "Simon?"

"Come in." Simon's baritone voice echoed through the space and down the corridor. His head was bent over some papers. The green marks all over the page made me think he was going through applications already. My throat felt like sandpaper.

"Sorry to bother you, Simon." I froze in the doorway.

The creases around his eyes deepened as he made his way to where I stood. "Wow, that is a dedicated social worker right there." He glanced at the clock on the wall. It was past six. "What brings you by at this hour?" He motioned to a couple of tub chairs.

"I know the deadline for this year's mentoring program is today..." I handed the neatly folded binder to him"...so I wanted to make sure I got this in before tomorrow." My throat burned. I stifled a cough.

"Can I offer you something to drink?" A mini fridge by Simon's desk offered sodas and bottles of water.

"Water, please."

Simon grabbed two bottles before settling back on his chair. "May I?" He handed me one, swapping it for my application. Sweat pooled down my back as Simon glanced over the nine-page plea. "That is an extensive application, April." He placed it on the coffee table in front of us. "Why don't you just tell me why you want to join the mentoring program?"

Oh, God. Hours typing the damn thing and now I have to articulate it.

Simon's piercing blue eyes stared through me. He waited, in silence, while the words crawled through my cloudy mind.

Fake it until you make it, April.

A large, stiff smile pasted over my face, I crossed my legs and placed a hand on my knee. If that wasn't the perfect picture of the committed mentee, I didn't know what else would be.

"I have been a social worker for five years; three of those were spent in this clinic. Every patient I see teaches me something about mental health, about recovery, and about myself." I took a deep breath. "However, in my current role, I have limited therapeutic opportunities. At times, it feels that social work is restricted to bureaucratic duties..."

Simon tilted his head sideways before raising an eyebrow.

Don't upset him! Or insult his department.

My hand covered my mouth. A grin covered his. When I hesitated, Simon encouraged me. "Don't stop. I've had these views since I took on the position. I want to hear what you have to say."

"It seems that the bulk of the therapy is done by psychology, which is completely fine, of course. They should..." I closed my eyes and cleared my throat.

"April, relax. It's just me and you, having a casual conversation." Simon leaned in. "Keep going."

"But what is being asked of social workers is ridiculous. It's bordering on de-skilling. Welfare assistants are trained to undertake basic psychosocial work, and if we hired them, it would free social workers for family therapy and general counselling."

"Tell me about your interest in therapies. What drives you to be so passionate?"

My breath hitched. The crossroad stared me in the face. I could either tell him the truth and make myself vulnerable, or lie. In the end, the truth was too powerful.

"I went through a traumatic loss when I was twelve. Nothing was available for many years, but when I was given access to support, it changed my life. I wouldn't be where I am today without the wonderful therapist who believed in me. She happened to be a social worker."

Simon leaned back in his chair, a warm smile on his face. He rested an ankle over his knee. "How do you think the program will help you?"

Finally, an easy question. I'd learned the answer by heart for the last three years.

"This is a once-in-a-lifetime opportunity to gain clinical counselling hours and professional development points. Participants leave the program eligible for multiple memberships and Medicare registration. And most importantly, it paves the way for social work recognition. I want to be part of this."

Well done, April. One question you didn't stuff up.

"I'm impressed. I won't lie." Simon lifted my application off the table and put it atop a pile of documents on the side. "It will be my pleasure to welcome you into my team."

Shivers crawled over my skin, the pounding in my chest increased, and my lips curled of their own volition. "Really? Are you serious?"

After three years of trying to fit in, Simon was finally giving me a chance. A positive current ran through me, and for a moment, I felt unstoppable.

Simon chuckled. "I am. I mean, it's a work in progress, and some of the cases are not the most therapeutic, but it will be great to have you onboard."

"Thank you. Really, thank you, Simon."

He grabbed a small folder from another pile on the table and gestured for me to open it.

It read: *Drug-diversion case. Jarryd Williams.*

"As I said, this one isn't rocket science. Six court-mandated drug counselling sessions. Psychoeducation, motivational interviewing, brief intervention... that type of stuff."

"Sounds great. Thank you."

"We'll talk about it more when the program officially begins; however, for all intents and purposes, the clients remain under the care of an accredited clinician. But as a mentee, you'll do most of the clinical work."

I handed the chart back to Simon, our fingers almost touching.

"I'll be your clinical supervisor, so you and I will meet on a regular basis to discuss cases and so forth. Sound okay with you?"

On the outside, I remained calm and nodded at my director.

Inside was a different story.

Also by S K Mason

THE HOPE ISLAND SERIES

Forbidden Promise

Reckless Attraction

Dangerous Love

Sinful Redemption

Acknowledgments

Thank you to my support crew who haven't stopped encouraging me. My PA Natasha, who I won't lie, is a God send. Kylie Kent, Naomi, Chris, Melissa Ridell, my coaches Keona, Ivica, and my business coach Sam. Of course, a massive thank you to my beta readers from the Romance Critique Club on Scribophile; Peyton James, Iris Black, Mina Jane, Janet Reid, and FC Chazer.

About the Author

I began writing stories in primary school, stories I would sell to my maternal grandmother, and stories she kept forever. Now, my paternal grandmother, an avid romance reader, would let me read her Harlequin collection over every summer, and soon my books took on a romance turn of their own!

Fast-forward thirty years later and SK Mason was born. A romance lover with a passion for "happily ever after" and pretty groovy ethical twists. In "real life", I mingle in the health sector, so don't be surprised that most of my books are inspired by these fun and intense settings.

When I'm not writing, I'm spending time with my family in Australia. My children are my life and together we cook, swim and ride our bikes. Life doesn't get better than that!"

Follow me on social media!

- www.skmasonauthor.com
- www.facebook.com/skmasonauthor
- www.instagram.com/skmasonauthor
- www.tiktok.com/skmasonauthor